Chicken Culprit

MOREWELLSON, LTD

Morewellson, Ltd.
P.O. Box 49726
Colorado Springs, CO 80949

ISBN: 978-0-9994402-0-9 (standard edition print)
      978-0-9994402-1-6 (epub)
      978-0-9994402-2-3 (large print)

This is a work of fiction. Names, characters, places, and incidents either are the product of the author's imagination or are used fictitiously, and any resemblance to actual persons, living or dead, business establishments, events, or locales is entirely coincidental.

Front Cover Illustration: Erika Parker Rogers
Publishing and Design Services: MartinPublishingServices.com

Chicken Culprit

A
BACKYARD FARMING
MYSTERY

BOOK 1

VIKKI WALTON

MOREWELLSON, LTD

Cast of Characters
(in order of appearance)

Anne Freemont: She seeks solace from her past in her new hometown of Carolan Springs.

Kandi Jenkins: A naïve and spirited young woman who thinks the best of everyone.

Ralph Rogers: A man whose temperament and actions cause angry confrontations.

Stewart Rogers: Ralph's nephew who's always turning up unexpectedly.

Everett Bradley: Town's police chief filling in as assisting agency for the sheriff's office.

Sam Powers: EMT and deputy coroner who befriends newcomer Anne.

Eliza de French: An Ethiopian woman whose beauty hides an ugly secret.

Hope Boswell: Doctor and herbalist who's come home to care for her ailing mother.

Faith Boswell: Dealing with early onset dementia, she still has what some call second sight.

Jeff Jenkins: Kandi's goal-oriented husband who often travels for work.

Sheriff Carson: A stony wall of shrewd insight into people.

Sorcha Smith: Bookstore owner who makes every man's head swivel.

Trust is like a sheet of paper; once it's crumpled, it is never viewed the same again.

Chapter One

Anne yawned and stretched her hands over her head. She unlocked the kitchen window, taking in a deep breath of crisp Colorado air and sighed loudly. No longer would she have to deal with divorce lawyers or Duke. She could finally live her life as she saw fit.

Anne surveyed her domain. Even though boxes cluttered every available space, it didn't matter. What she cared about was that it was all hers. While the work ahead might seem daunting, the prospect of transforming the old Victorian house didn't deter Anne.

She poured herself a cup of coffee, both hands cradling the mug, before deciding to drink it out on the back porch. Rays of sunshine had risen about the copse at the back of her property, and its golden warmth welcomed the day. Raising the mug to her mouth, Anne took a much-needed sip of the hot morning brew.

"Stop! Stop!" A woman's voice carried over from the other yard.

Anne sloshed coffee onto her chambray shirt. "Shoot!" She set her cup down on the railing. The liquid, now cold, seeped through to her skin.

"Stop!" The piercing scream came again. This was no couple's tiff or "you forgot your lunch" yell. Anne lurched down the steps and across the yard, striding over to the stand of lilacs which separated the two yards. As she drew closer, a woman's high-pitched voice could be heard pleading. A much deeper voice—a man's—was muffled in contrast.

Last night's rain made her flip-flops slip on the spongy ground. She cautiously rounded the stand of lilacs and stared at the scene before her.

A petite young woman with fiery red hair stood facing a much taller older gentleman. She held something red in her hands. It moved.

A chicken.

The man gripped an axe with his right hand. With his left, he reached out and took hold of the chicken's neck.

As Anne watched, open-mouthed, the woman reached up and grabbed the axe handle. The ruddy-faced man stood unyielding, his left hand wrapped securely around the chicken's neck.

The chicken didn't look happy either.

"Let go, Kandi, before someone gets hurt."

The young woman released the axe. "Fine, but you let go of Rusty."

Rusty must be the Rhode Island Red Kandi clutched in her left hand.

"Kandi, I've had it. I told you the last time to keep your cotton-picking chickens out of my garden. Now look at what she's done." The man released the chicken's neck and pointed.

Anne took a few steps into the yard to see where he pointed.

The torn remains of a gorgeous heirloom Brandywine tomato left no doubt as to the culprit.

Anne took a few more steps into the yard to make her presence known. The scene made it clear that no one was in danger, except for maybe the chicken.

"Please, Ralph," Kandi whimpered, "I'll make sure she doesn't get out of the run again."

The chicken squawked and struggled to break free from Kandi's tight grip.

"You've told me this before, young lady." He reached for the chicken. "Come on, Fricassee. I could use me a plate of chicken cutlets for dinner tonight."

"Over my dead body, you will!" Kandi stepped back.

Valiantly protesting being dinner, the chicken struck out with a poor attempt to peck at the man.

Anne sneezed.

The pair turned to face her.

Discovered, Anne sheepishly stepped further into the yard. She raised her hand in a slight wave.

"Hi, I'm Anne. I just moved—"

"You've got to help me!" The woman jogged over to Anne and pointed at the man. "He's going to murder Rusty!" She held the chicken up for display so there would be no doubt who she meant.

The man advanced toward Anne, still clutching said 'chicken-murder-weapon-of-choice.'

"Hi. I'm Ralph. Mr. Rogers. I'm your neighbor."

Anne struggled not to laugh. She looked from axe-bearing Mr. Rogers to the young woman to the chicken frantic to escape. It wasn't a good day in the neighborhood.

"Hi. I'm Kandi. I live over there." She used the chicken to point across the yard to the next property. "I keep chickens in case you want fresh eggs."

While Ralph stood silent, Kandi continued. "Did you move in yesterday? I was so excited when the house sold. Are you—" She tightened her grip on Rusty who squirmed to break free.

"Enough." Ralph's deep baritone stopped Kandi's questioning.

He advanced. The axe's sharp edge gleamed in his hand.

Anne stepped back and her flip-flops sucked into the mud. She fought to regain purchase but found only unstable ground. Struggling to remain upright and keep her footing, she spun her arms in a tilt-a-whirl motion.

Kandi let go of the chicken. Mr. Rogers chucked the axe to the ground and they both reached for Anne.

Their efforts were in vain.

Gravity won.

Anne landed with a thud in a large mound of fresh, earthy, wet compost. She may have laughed it off at twenty, but falls weren't as funny as they used to be. She stared up at the two maniacs.

The man let out a loud laugh. "Welcome to the neighborhood!"

"Very funny." Anne shifted sideways, placing one jeaned knee in the pile for stability. Wet and cold seeped through her pants. She fought a losing battle as decaying leaves, rotting vegetables, and who knew what else shifted and sunk beneath her.

Her endeavors to pull free from the muck were getting her nowhere. Exasperation grew. "A little help here would be appreciated." Her voice rose.

Ralph held out his calloused hand. Thankfully, sans axe.

Anne grabbed it. With a firm pull, he yanked her up, swaying a bit as he sought to remain upright on solid ground.

As Kandi grasped at Anne's other arm, Ralph turned his head. "Where's that chicken? Kan-di! It's in my garden again! I'll kill it for sure this time!" He dropped Anne's arm and grabbed the axe from the ground.

Kandi also dropped Anne's arm and took off after Ralph.

Anne's foot sunk once again in the compost pile, and she fell back into the damp muck.

Frustrated with this new pair of neighbors, Anne pulled herself up and began crawling out of the compost heap.

"Don't hurt her," Kandi implored. "I promise I'll make sure she doesn't get in your tomatoes again. I'll even go right now and buy you some tomatoes to replace the ones she's ruined."

"Are you nuts? If I wanted store-bought no-taste tomatoes, I'd buy them." He glowered down at the young woman.

Kandi bristled. She stretched herself to her full five-foot frame and placed her hands on her hips, Wonder-Woman style. Then, before Ralph could react, she rushed over and scooped up the errant chicken. The young woman sprinted toward her yard, the chicken's head bobbing with the movement.

As she rounded the corner, she turned back to the finally upright Anne. "Nice to meet you, Anne!" Kandi waved.

Anne waved back. A piece of romaine stuck to her hand.

Oh, joy. What have I gotten myself into?

Finally freed from the compost quicksand, Anne said goodbye to Ralph. She headed home carrying her flip-flops, now utterly useless. Her shirt was wet. Her pants were wet. Why not her feet too?

The screen door slapped the frame behind her as she entered the kitchen. She used her hip to shut the main door. Dropping the shoes in a trash bin, Anne quickly shucked off her damp shirt, carrying it with her down the short passage to her bedroom.

Her muscles ached. Between the moving of boxes yesterday and today's spill, soreness now made itself known. She pulled out a piece of lettuce—no, arugula—stuck in her hair. Gazing down at her grimy hands caked with dirt, she grimaced.

Working hands. That's what Duke—her ex-husband—had called them.

She thought back to his chiding remarks. "How am I supposed to feel when you don't even make yourself presentable? Look at Stu's wife. Now *that's* a woman."

Anne studied her hands. Gone were the sculpted manicured nails. Turning on the tap, she scrubbed at her hands with the intensity of a heart surgeon. Tears flowed. Her hands, now red from her efforts, throbbed. She stepped back from the sink and threw the nail brush as hard as she could at the bathroom window.

Unfortunately for her, the bathroom window was closed. She'd shut it when the rain started last night.

The plastic missile bounced back off the window and hit her on the shoulder. "Ow!" The tears morphed into laughter at her own stupidity.

Though her stomach rumbled, begging for food, a bath was the first order of business. No telling what had been in that compost muck. She loved compost, worms, and other critters, just not on her person. She bent down and turned on the bath faucet, hoping the hot water had generated enough heat overnight for a long soak.

A loud knocking on the back door interrupted the process.

Maybe they'll go away. Wait—is anything supposed to be hooked up today?

She begrudgingly turned off the faucet and grabbed the old raincoat she'd worn last night from the back of the shower door. Should that have been a clue of a stormy beginning to her new life?

She shoved her matted brown hair behind her ears. The postponement of warm water on her sore backside elicited a sigh of disappointment.

Walking toward the kitchen, she glimpsed a tall young man standing on the porch. She cracked the back door open. "Can I help you?"

He pointed to the lilac bushes. "I'm Ralph's nephew. Stewart. Next door. He's real sorry about you falling into his compost heap. Last night's rain made the ground real slippery back there."

No kidding. Her clenched fist gripped the coat tightly, but she replied, "No harm, no foul."

Foul—fowl. She chuckled.

His eyebrow raised in question.

"You see, no foul. This all began because of a chicken, fowl, get it?…Oh, never mind."

"Um, okay."

His dismissive demeanor rankled. But she didn't want to start off on the wrong foot with her neighbor. She giggled a bit thinking about her lost footing. *Oh man, I'm really tired.*

His appraising look left no doubt he thought her a kook. "Anyway…he wanted to give you these as an apology." He motioned to a crate of beautiful vegetables that sat at his feet.

Stewart continued, "This is a great place you got here. Good bones. I know you'll like it. My uncle said you might need some handyman help. I do some carpentry and such. General stuff. Be glad to give you a quote." He patted the door frame. "You can't do better than these old Victorians."

Anne didn't respond. Though she felt the same about the beautiful old home, the less she said, the quicker he'd leave.

"Well, anyway, Uncle Ralph asked me to give that to you." He motioned in the direction of the box. "Sorry to hear about your fall. Welcome to Carolan Springs." Turning, he bounded down the steps while fixing a baseball cap back on his head.

Anne stepped out onto the porch. As she watched, Stewart sprinted beyond the lilacs. Now alone, she picked up the crate and brought it inside to the old oak table. Peeking at the goodies, it didn't look like anything needed refrigeration. It could wait for her to take her bath.

Footsteps crunched on the gravel out to her drive. *Did he forget something?*

She buttoned her coat before turning to see the young woman from this morning's fiasco grinning at her from the open doorway.

Not waiting for approval, the woman entered the kitchen. "Oh wow, you do look, well…" She colored slightly. "Not to be mean, but you don't look so good."

"Falling into a compost heap will do that to you." Anne brushed back a stray lock of sticky hair from her face. She looked down at her hand and saw a piece of strawberry. "By the way, good for you for standing up to that guy. Some young people might have been intimidated by him."

"Ahh, he's okay. Plus, I'm twenty-four."

"You are? Wow. You look much younger," Anne quipped.

"I get that a lot." Kandi looked around the kitchen. "Don't you just love this old house?" She laughed a childlike laugh that couldn't help but make Anne smile. "Oh, of course you do. You bought it!"

She focused her eyes intently on Anne. "Seriously though. You look, *like*, bad. I don't know if you know but the back of your head has, *like*, what might be a moldy strawberry or some other gross stuff in it.

Anne shuddered. Suddenly, she was itchy everywhere.

"Anyway, I came over because I figure you need help. You being old and all."

Old and all? Had this twit just called her old? She was only forty for heaven's sake. Okay, forty-four and a half, but who's counting?

She looked at the girl. Innocence radiated from her face. She hadn't meant to be cruel or mean. She had only been stating a fact. Did she look old? Anne knew that the stress of the last few years had taken their toll. Maybe it had been more than she thought.

Kandi continued, "I thought you might like some help unpacking after your fall. Plus, I kind of, *like*, owe you since you saved Rusty." She glanced at Anne's raincoat. "Are you going out? I don't think that's, *like*, such a good idea."

Before Anne could respond, Kandi rushed out to the back porch and returned holding a basket. "Look!" Like a toddler holding up a present, Kandi extended her arms to showcase a basketful of eggs. "These are from my girls—my chickens. You may not know this about chickens, but these are, *like*, the best eggs you'll ever taste. Bright orange yolks. They look like you've added cheese to the eggs." She grinned.

Kandi glanced at the crate on the table. "Hey, is that,

like, some of Ralph's veggies?" She pulled items from the box. "Um, here are some peppers, onions, and even some of his prized mushrooms. He's got a secret spot down the trail that leads from his place into the forest. You've, *like*, scored the jackpot."

Anne raised a hand to rub her forehead. This woman and all her *likes* made her head hurt.

Kandi gazed intently at Anne. "I can see you're super tired. Yep, what you need is a good homemade frittata. My Jeff says I'm the best cook in, *like*, the whole county. How about you go take a shower and by the time you're done, I'll have the food ready."

Anne wanted to strangle the young woman and be done with it. She debated whether Kandi could be a frittata-making serial killer and as her stomach rumbled again, decided she'd chance it.

"Okay," she mumbled. Food cooked by someone else, killer or no, sounded divine.

As Kandi set about pulling items from the box, Anne headed off to the shower. She was tired. More than she realized. As Anne shucked off her coat, a light knock sounded on the bathroom door, causing her to jump. Oh geez, how could she have forgotten to lock her bedroom door? With a complete stranger in her kitchen no less. She must be far more tired than she'd realized.

"You okay in there? Need any help?" Kandi's youthful voice came through.

"No, I've got my walker in here with me." Anne grinned at her own quip.

"Okay. Good." The young woman's voice rang out.

Anne rolled her eyes. "I was being facetious. I don't have a walker!"

"Well, how long will it take to be facetious? I want to put the frittata in the oven and don't want it getting cold."

This woman has to be dumber than a brick. Oh geez, how mean. Anne gripped the sides of the sink, her pale arms freckled by the sun, and scrutinized her sad, tired eyes in the mirror. *What's wrong with you, Anne?*

"I won't be long. You can go ahead and put it in."

"Great. I'll just finish putting your dishes away." Kandi shuffled away from the door, quietly humming to herself.

Anne grimaced. If there was anything worse than moving into a house, it had to be someone else deciding the best place for things. She went to grab her coat and then decided against it. She'd take a quick shower and stop the young woman before she got too far into it. Anne turned this way and that, inspecting her hair in the mirror for any errant pieces of lettuce or other compost material. While happy not to find any more fruit or vegetables, she did notice strands of gray that stood out against the darker strands. *Am I old? When did that happen? Nah.*

Finally in the shower, the warm water cascading down her back, Anne paused to think. Moving at forty-four had proven physically challenging. Twenty years ago she wouldn't have had these aches and pains. But with the constant strain of her marriage, the accident—no, she wouldn't think about that—and little exercise, it was no wonder fatigue hit so hard. Well, it wouldn't last for long. She couldn't—no, she wouldn't—let it. She knew her own strength now.

Emerging from the shower, she opened a box marked *herbal*. Inside, she found the jar of comfrey salve and applied it to her scraped elbows and hands. The compost had been soft, but she'd scratched them on the bushes as she'd fallen. Applying the soothing ointment on her skin brought comfort and she sighed deeply. Even the short shower had done its magic.

Wiping the fog from the mirror, Anne checked her face for any dirt or scratches she'd missed. Even with so much time spent in the garden, she'd retained her pretty peaches-and-cream complexion. She combed the remaining tangles from her hair before pulling it into a top knot. She wrapped the towel back around her, wishing she'd brought clothes into the bathroom with her.

She yawned. Between working late, poor sleep, and this morning's fall, it was no wonder she was so tired. Passing into her bedroom, she looked longingly at the bed. She wanted to climb back under the covers and sleep for two days.

Would Kandi get the hint if I never came out?

Her stomach growled again. She took in a deep breath to fortify herself.

"Okay, we can do this."

"Did you say something?" Kandi called to her.

Anne had forgotten that her room—the old maid's quarters—was so close to the kitchen.

She tried to make her voice sound cheery. "Nothing.

Just talking to myself. Please, don't feel you need to stay on my account."

"Oh, no worries. I have, *like*, all the time in the world. Plus, I want to get to know my new neighbor."

Drat. Anne pulled on a soft cotton shift and headed for the kitchen.

Kandi turned as Anne entered the room. "Wow. You look like one of those hippie chicks. Very cool."

"Thanks." Anne motioned to the counters, now completely free of clutter. "I appreciate your help but, seriously, you don't need to do anything."

"Not a problem. I have the same kitchen arrangement so I got most of it done while you were in the shower." Kandi smiled up at Anne.

"Thanks again." *Now I'll have to redo everything. What is the matter with you? This girl is trying to help you.*

"Are you okay?" Kandi's worried face came into view.

"I'm sorry. I've been very tired lately. Probably the move and then the fall this morning."

Kandi kept staring. "Um, okay. If you say so." She held up two pieces of bread. "I didn't see any bread so I ran home and got some. Rye or spelt? Or if you're like me, you have a hard time choosing. I'll make both." She looked around. "Toaster?"

Anne grabbed the toaster from a box in the adjoining room. "What can I do to help?"

"It's about ready. Sit down and relax." Kandi pointed to a chair.

As Kandi worked, Anne watched the young woman. She stood at least four to six inches shorter than Anne.

Her toned arms revealed a strong workout regimen. Her hair, a brilliant red, matched the bright lipstick she wore.

Kandi's freckled face, along with dimples when she smiled, explained Anne's earlier impression of her youth. Yet strangely, the way she took command of the situation made her seem much older than her years. While the girl may not have had much education, she was certainly accomplished in the commonsense arts.

As Kandi moved to take the frittata from the oven, her snug T-shirt rode up. Anne glimpsed the tattoo on Kandi's back. It was simply the word *Past*.

What did that mean? She felt more intrigued by her and what the tattoo meant. Anne fiddled with a paper napkin on the table. She had to be cordial no matter how tired or sore she felt. When was the last time anyone had taken such good care of her? She smiled up at Kandi.

Kandi returned the smile. "I see you looking at my hair. Like it? It's candy apple red. Get it? Like Kandi is my name—"

"I get it. Cute."

"I told Cheryl to do something fun with it and she did! Jeff hates it, well…" A cloud passed over her features before she brightened again. "Never mind. Isn't it fun?"

Anne nodded.

Kandi laid out the table. From a bag she must have retrieved while Anne was in the shower, she pulled a jar of homemade jam, a slab of butter, cream, and a carafe.

Please, oh patron saint of tired peoples, let that be coffee.

Kandi poured the steaming hot coffee into a mug and placed one in front of Anne and one at her own place.

Then she cut the frittata and placed it on a plate with the toast.

The smells of the rich coffee and cheesy frittata wafted in the air. Anne took in a deep breath and sighed contentedly. She'd been doing that a lot lately. The move had been a smart decision.

"I'm feeling very spoiled. Thanks for everything." She took a swig of the hot brew.

Setting the plate in front of Anne, Kandi sat down.

"Aren't you eating?"

"Nope, I'm on a new diet. Jeff's been kidding me about getting a bit chubby."

A bit chubby? The girl was probably a minus-zero in size—if there was such a thing.

Kandi went on. "You know, got to keep the figure. It's the three-one-zero diet. Heard of it?" The young woman cocked her head to the side, her four earrings tinkling as she did so. She took a swig of black coffee. "So you eat three meals one day, then only one meal the next day, and then no food on the third day, then repeat. Plus they give you a huge list of foods not to eat so you don't even have to think about it." She gazed longingly at Anne's plate.

"Let me guess," Anne replied. "None of what's on this plate is okay to eat. Look, there's nothing wrong with your figure. You're the perfect size for your height and you're pretty. Not to mention that you have a natural talent around the kitchen and you're kind to strangers."

"Really?" Kandi jumped from her seat, darted around the table, and hugged Anne, who groaned from the strong embrace. She must have twisted something in her back when she'd fallen. Then the stupid adolescent display with the nailbrush. She'd kick herself for the outburst but that would hurt even more. With Kandi returning to her seat, Anne massaged the spot the nailbrush had hit.

Anne focused on her coffee cup, pretending not to notice Kandi discreetly wipe tears from her eyes. After Kandi composed herself, Anne spoke. "Here's the thing, Kandi. I eat on my own enough. If you don't eat, I don't eat."

For the love of all that is good, please work.

Anne shoved the plate away. She raised an eyebrow in a silent "well?" and waited.

Kandi frowned, the internal debate evident in her face. "I don't want you to go without because of me." She grabbed a plate and filled it.

Anne let out her breath. She pulled the plate to her and took a bite of the egg dish. The frittata, perfectly cooked, was delightfully light and fluffy. The onions, peppers, and mushrooms worked together in an exquisite sensory experience. The bread's heavy texture provided the ideal complement for the creamy butter and homemade blackberry jam.

"This is delicious, Kandi. You *are* a wonderful cook."

Kandi deflected the compliment by shrugging her shoulders. "I've been cooking since I was ten."

Ten! Curiouser and curiouser. Anne stared at the young girl.

Seeing sadness pass over Kandi's face, Anne didn't respond. "So what's the thing with my neighbor—Ralph, isn't it?"

Kandi brightened up. "Yes. Rotten Ralph. He's so mean." She took a swig of coffee before continuing. "My girls don't mean any harm. They're just, *like*, you know, chickens. And they like his tomatoes. It's not like he can't grow more. Though we do have a super short growing season. But nooooooo—he's like"—she stood and imitated a stern male voice, "—I'm going to kill your chicken if you let it come over here anymore."

Anne stifled a chuckle as Kandi plopped back down in her chair.

Kandi took a quick bite of toast before continuing. "He's so mean to everybody. I don't know why, but if he, *like*, ever hurts one of my girls, I'll kill him!" She stabbed her fork into the frittata.

Anne shook her head. The girl's constant use of the word *like* drove her crazy. She felt like responding in kind "So, *like*, he hates your, *like*, chickens, and he isn't very nice, *like*." Instead she felt a tug on her heart for this part-woman, part-child.

"Listen, Kandi, I appreciate everything you've done for me. I truly do. But I was up almost all last night getting things unloaded. I apologize but I'm feeling a bit cranky, and I think I need to ask if you'll excuse me so I can get some rest."

Kandi nodded. "I can tell. You go get in bed and I'll clean up." Kandi gathered the now-empty plates.

"Thanks. Really. But you don't need to do that. You've done enough. I'll take care of it when I get up."

Kandi set down the dishes. "You are sore. I can tell. I'll take care of everything." She pointed to the back bedroom, commanding, "Now, go!"

Too tired to argue with this little spitfire, Anne nodded and shuffled to the bedroom. This time she locked the door behind her. She wasn't sure if she wanted to hug the young woman or strangle her, but she was simply too tired to deal with it.

Tomorrow would be better for murder.

Chapter Two

Lilac scent wafted through the open bedroom window. Anne fumbled for her phone on the bedside table.

Two o'clock.

Great. So much for getting anything accomplished today.

Anne stared at the ceiling. Had she dreamed the morning escapades? No. She'd met Rotten Ralph, Kandi the Conversationalist, and Ralph's nephew, Stewart the Smug.

She groaned as she forced herself to sit up. The wrinkled dress bunched around her legs, and she pulled to untangle its folds. Maybe Kandi had left the coffee. Anne shuffled to the kitchen, a loud yawn escaping from her mouth.

Dishes from the morning's breakfast were washed and put away. On the table stood a mason jar full of sunflowers. A handwritten note on pink paper lay in front of it.

Dear Anne,

> *Came by, but you were still sleeping. Didn't want to wake you. I told everyone about you moving in, so they all wanted to contribute. In the fridge you'll find some of Marge's goat cheese, milk from Sonny's, and apples from the orchard down the road. Also some honey from Bill, pickled veggies from Velma, and some elderberry cordial from old lady Marie. Can you believe it? Even Rotten Ralph contributed some of his precious tomatoes. I could kill that man! Oh, Stew says if you need anything, let him know. Kandi XXOO*

Anne set the note down and opened the previously empty fridge. It now contained delightful goodies.

How in the world did I not hear all this going on?

Tears gathered. She sat down as they rolled down her cheeks. She'd been horrible to that girl, critiquing everything she'd done or said. Why?

What's the matter with you? This is the second time you've cried today. Pull yourself together woman.

She took a deep breath. But the tears grew to deep gut-wrenching sobs.

I'm going crazy. That's what. I'm finally free from Duke and his demands and now *I decide to go crazy?*

Wearily, she headed to the bedroom. She didn't even remove her slippers before launching herself onto the bed and back into a deep sleep.

By the time Anne woke, the room was cloaked in dappled shade from the tree outside her window. 5:30. She'd make some coffee and then get at least a few boxes unpacked.

Anne made the same slow shuffle once more to the kitchen.

Her back door stood open.

She didn't remember leaving it open. She moved to close it when a shadowy figure on the porch startled her. She screamed.

Kandi stepped out of the gloom.

Anne flipped on the switch, bathing the dark porch with light. "What are you doing? You scared me half to death!"

Kandi giggled. "Don't be a-scared, silly. No one, *like*, locks their doors here. We all keep a lookout for strangers, and, *like*, probably eighty percent of the townsfolk have guns. Hunters, don'tcha know."

Kandi laughed and then became serious. "Bears are sometimes spotted around here before hibernation. But it's the mountain lions that have most people armed. You know, *like*, just in case."

Anne shivered at the idea of danger so close. She'd known moving to a small Colorado mountain town would take getting used to, but this was more than she'd considered. Bears. Mountain lions. She peered into the gathering gloom and deep forest at the edge of her property.

Something was moving—no running—in the brush. Anne called out, "It's a bear!"

Kandi turned and squinted. She laughed. "Oh, that's just a runner. There's a trail back there. People walk and run it all the time. It runs along our area and out to the lake."

She pushed past a shaken Anne. "I came by to, *like*, look in and see if you needed more help. You weren't up yet, so I came out here to enjoy the view.

The young woman thrust out her neck, squinting. "You, *like*, don't look so good."

"I'm pretty sure you've already told me that once today. Thank you very much." Ugh. There, she was doing it again. Snippy. Anne pulled out a chair and sat down.

"No. I mean you look sick. Do you feel bad?"

Now that she'd mentioned it, Anne didn't feel well. She'd attributed her fatigue and need for sleep to moving stress, all the work yesterday, plus the nasty tumble into the compost. But maybe there *was* more to it. . .

No, too many projects. No time to be sick.

"I'm just tired." She ran her fingers through the hair that had fallen loose.

The young woman tilted her head to the right again, a cockatoo with flaming red feathers sprouting atop her head.

More like a cuckoo bird that drives you crazy on the hour.

Anne smiled up at the girl who grinned back.

"Okay, that does it. 'Get your shoes on, Sally,' cause we're headed to the city."

"Um, what?"

She swept past Anne, making a beeline to the mudroom. The small room had most likely been the scullery in its day. Anne followed her out on the porch. Kandi picked up a pair of clogs Anne had worn last night. They were covered in mud and muck. She thrust them at Anne. "Here, stick these on."

"I have to comb my hair and put on something else—"

"No time." Kandi grabbed her hand and half-dragged Anne down the steps. Once they reached the gravel driveway, she motioned to Anne. "You go round to the front. I'll meet you in the truck." Kandi sprinted past the lilac hedge. "I'm taking you to our local doc."

Still too sleepy and disoriented to argue, Anne made her way around to the front of the house. Maybe she had the flu. She hadn't been sleeping well. She felt like she had a fever and the next minute, chills. Going to a doctor wasn't her priority, but she needed to figure out why she was feeling at odds and not herself.

Reaching the street, Anne spied Stewart stomping away from Ralph's house. Scowling, he strode over to a van of dubious running potential. Painted an ugly khaki green, bondo plaster covered much of the fender area. The van puffed out black smoke as it grudgingly started up. The vehicle roared to life, and its tires squealed as Stewart reversed, barely missing Ralph's mailbox.

As he left, Kandi pulled up in a shiny red Dodge pickup. Anne had barely closed the door when Kandi shifted into gear. "Geez, I wonder what's got Stewart all hot under the collar? But, whatever. I called Hope, and she's agreed to take a look at you. You're one lucky woman. I think it's because you're new to town. Plus I begged her to see you." She winked at Anne.

Anne smiled back at the young woman. "Thanks, Kandi."

Kandi continued babbling, though Anne sat lost in her own thoughts. Every once in a while, words would come through—herbs, Main Street, mama, witch—wait, what? Before she could ask Kandi to repeat herself, they turned onto Main Street.

This delightful avenue with its local shops had sold Anne on living here. When she had seen the town's name—Carolan Springs—in the realtor ad, it had felt like a sign. Nobody called her by her full name, Carole Anne, but it still felt like two halves coming together to make a whole.

Small compared to most cities, this quaint place of around four thousand had instantly soothed her hurting soul. Choosing to settle in a town with one main street and three major cross streets had made her happy. For the first time in a very long time, she'd felt at peace.

Even better, she wasn't that far from Main Street. No tract homes here. Rows of Victorian-style houses dotted the wide, tree-lined roads. Her own little cul-de-sac of such magnificent homes, reminiscent of an era long past, had made her decision to move here even easier. She could finally live in an older home like she preferred instead of the modern glass and metal monstrosity Duke had insisted on during their marriage. Even better, they could have easily walked to town, instead of making the ten-minute drive. Trails intersected throughout the area providing a way for people to walk, run, or bike in the beautiful Colorado weather.

Kandi parked in front of a shop with a soft butter-yellow awning over the windows. The awning's color echoed other shops down the street. Each shop presented its persona through its choice of designs and fonts. On this shop, a vines-and-flowers motif had been used with the words *Herbal Lotions and Potions* printed in a fluid script.

"Come on. She's waiting." Kandi beckoned, then stopped, glancing toward her left as a woman's voice carried over to them.

"Who would have done this most horrible deed?" A statuesque woman, her skin the color of coffee with cream, stood a few spots up the street behind a silver BMW.

The woman reached down with the grace of a ballerina and picked something off the street. Straightening, she turned toward Kandi and Anne. She strode toward them like a model owning the runway in her Ferragamos.

"Hel-lo." Her exotic voice flowed with the enunciation of each syllable. The woman nodded at Anne, the straightened locks of her bobbed haircut cupped her chin.

Anne cringed when she remembered her uncombed bed hair, her wrinkled and stained dress, and her muddy clogs. Even though she wanted to crawl into a gutter, far, far away from this magnificent creature, Anne felt no judgment in her eyes. The woman smiled She smiled back.

Instinctively, Anne liked this woman of propriety

and beauty, even though they couldn't have been more different in appearance or manner.

"Hi, Eliza." Kandi slung her red purse onto her shoulder.

"Kandi," she said in a lyrical, British-sounding accent, "did you happen to see who may have damaged my vehicle?" She held out a piece of red plastic. "I'd left my car in town during my trip and it must have been hit sometime today.

"Sorry, Eliza. We just arrived. What happened?"

"It appears someone has backed into my automobile, and, unfortunately, left no notice of insurance or contact information. As you can see my taillight is broken and my bumper damaged."

"Let's take a look." Kandi led the way and crouched to look at the fender. "Whoever did it, looks like the car was green. So that means it could be, um, Ms. Alice— you know her daughter's been after her to quit driving— Pete Owens, he drives a green Dodge, Lori Conner has a green Focus, and, like, who else, I remember, someone else, um, oh yeah, Rott—Ralph Rogers. You should call the police, and, like, make a report."

Carolan Springs might be small but it has to have more than four green cars. What is Kandi thinking?

Anne rubbed her arms as a chill embraced her. These days she was either hot or cold. Maybe she did have the flu.

"Most astute. Thank you, my darling Kandi. I'm sure that whoever did it may not have known they had hit my car. I will determine the best course of action I should take at this point."

She turned to Anne. "I apologize for my lack of manners. I was—am—in such a state. Please let me be formally introduced to you. My name is Eliza de French."

"Nice to meet you, Eliza. Anne Freemont." She stuck out her hand, which looked short and stubby compared to Eliza's long fingers, which were encased in a zebra-striped glove. The designer accessory coordinated with the blouse the woman wore underneath her couture suit jacket.

I remember well-made clothing. But I'll take simple clothes and happiness any day.

"It is my pleasure to meet you. I must not keep you from your appointment. I hope we will meet again under more pleasant circumstances." She sashayed back to her vehicle.

"That is one beautiful woman," Anne said aloud to herself.

"Yes, and she's always very nice too." Kandi motioned her to follow.

Anne followed as Kandi spoke over her shoulder, "We'll have to go this way because Hope has closed up shop for the day. Come on." She moved toward a narrow passage between the two buildings. They arrived at a side door painted bright purple. Vibrant yellow stars sparkled against the dark background, while a smiling moon looked down on them from an upper corner. Kandi rapped on the door and waited.

The door opened to reveal an elderly woman, even shorter than Kandi, whose gray hair cascaded over one shoulder in a long braid. She wore a flowing orange caftan and turquoise slipper shoes. A big silver necklace and bracelet with the same gem completed the outfit. If Eliza's smile had shown a gracious kindness, this woman's emanated peace.

"Hi, Miss Faith." Kandi gave the woman a light kiss.

The woman called out, "Hope, your young friends are here." The woman disappeared through another door where Anne glimpsed a popular reality show on the television.

A woman appeared, wiping her hands on a paper towel. She stood about Anne's height, just shy of five-foot-six, and her chopped brown hair lay close to her head. Her russet eyes sparkled, and her face glowed with health. She wore no makeup or jewelry except for a quartz crystal pendant around her neck. "Hi. You must be Anne. I'm Hope." She held Anne's hand in both of her own.

"Hello. Nice to meet you. Sorry to intrude—" Anne replied.

"Not intruding. Right, Hope?" Kandi interjected. "You go ahead. I'm off to the bathroom and a quick visit with Miss Faith."

Hope beckoned to Anne to follow her into the next room. "Okay, so let's have a look at you." Hope stared at Anne's face. "Would you stick your tongue out, please?" Hope continued her cursory examination, asking Anne questions as she went along. She washed her hands, faced shelving full of jars and boxes, and spoke to herself. "Yes, exactly."

Exactly what? She heard the door open and turned to see Kandi had rejoined them.

Kandi sat down in a straight-back chair in the corner

and lifted her hand over her mouth. Hope laughed at Anne's confusion about Kandi's antics. "Kandi knows that I need people to be quiet so I can concentrate during exams." She smiled at Kandi. "That's more of a challenge for some people than others."

Kandi laughed heartily, then clamped her hands back over her mouth.

"Now we just need hear no evil and see no evil." At Anne's remark, they all burst out in laughter, easing the tension that permeated the room.

Hope returned to her task and moved from one area to another, adding herbs to a small container. From a woodstove in the corner, she took a teapot and poured water into a cup. After Hope added the herbal brew to the cup, a fragrant aroma filled the air.

She turned over a tea timer, the sand pouring through to the bottom. As the last bit of sand fell through on the timer, she removed the tea ball and handed the steaming cup to Anne. "Drink."

Anne took a sip. It had a bitter taste but also a sweet note at the end. "What—"

"No talking until you finish. And no need to hurry. Take your time. We'll wait." She motioned Kandi to join her and the two left the room.

Anne sank back into the overstuffed chair. The tea's warmth soothed and calmed her. She'd almost finished the cup when Hope returned.

"So," began Hope, plunking herself down on a rolling stool, "tired, weepy, brain fog, missed periods?" Anne nodded as Hope continued. "And when did the fall happen?"

Anne stared at her. This woman must be a psychic. "I…I—" Anne tried to gather her thoughts. Definitely weepy. Tired. Forgetful.

Hope continued. "How long have you been going through menopause?"

"Wha—I'm not…noooo." She shook her head. "Am I?"

Hope patted her hand. "Yes. It affects each woman differently but we all experience the change when we move from fertility to crone."

She just called me a crone. Anne's anger bubbled. She started to rise.

"Yep, you've got it. Indignant over little things. By the way, crone isn't a derogatory term. It's just you coming into the age of wisdom. How do you feel, by the way?"

"Better." Anne relaxed back into the chair.

"Great. I wanted to test out that herbal combination before I gave you some to take with you." She rolled the stool away from the chair and stood up. Anne rose and set the cup down on the adjacent table. Hope handed Anne a bag of herbal tea mix.

"You need to come back and see me. We'll take a more detailed medical history, have some blood work done, and"—she squeezed Anne's arm—"get you some hormonal help. As for your fall, take a long bath with Epsom salts and use this." She grabbed a packet from under the counter marked *arnica.* "You'll feel much better tomorrow."

"How did you know I fell?"

She smiled. "The old-fashioned way. Kandi told me. Plus, you're limping a bit."

She then hugged her, which made Anne tear up again. Hope pulled back and looked into Anne's face, "Menopause."

Anne had expected change, but not quite like this. That set her to some real crying.

Anne tore off the calendar page. Had it already been almost a month? She smiled as she poured steaming coffee into her mug. As she had done on almost every morning since arriving, she marveled at the lovely forest view through her kitchen window. The sun cast a beautiful glow over the backyard as it welcomed the day. Last night's rain had made everything clean and fresh. Though the first few weeks had been a bit hectic, things were finally coming together and many boxes were now empty of their contents. Pushing up her sweater sleeves, Anne added cream to her cup. Cupping the mug in both hands, she took a sip. Anne sighed, content with life.

She set the cup on the counter so she could open the window wider. As it moved up the track, Anne heard Kandi's voice from Ralph's yard.

"Stop! Nooooo, stop!"

The rebel hen must have gotten out of the run—again. Ralph isn't going to be happy.

Let the axe fall where it may. She had no intention of heading over and joining the melee this time. If it was on a chicken's neck, so be it. She took another swig of the welcome morning brew and waited for the exchange between Kandi and Ralph.

Instead only the whisper of wind came through the window.

Too quiet.

The hairs on her arm stood up. She cocked her ear toward the window. No sound. She stood still, listening. Her stomach knotted.

A piercing scream. *Kandi.*

The distress within the scream shocked Anne. The mug slipped from her hand and broke on the sink edge. Coffee splattered on the counter and floor. Without a moment's hesitation, Anne dashed out the back door and sprinted across the yard.

Kandi's cries grew more frantic. "No, no. Help! Somebody! Help!"

Ralph must have killed the chicken. *Ralph, it's just tomatoes. If you killed Kandi's chicken, I'm going to kill you.*

Anne sprinted across the yard. As she rounded the hedge, she stopped short.

On her knees at the edge of the compost pile, Kandi rocked back and forth, staring down at her hands. Blood stained her palms. Her beige pants, now dark with horrific markings, revealed where she'd tried to wipe blood off her hands.

Anne gasped when she saw Ralph on his back in the compost pile, staring unseeing into the sky, his shirt saturated in blood.

Chapter Three

"Kandi." Anne took a step forward. Their eyes met. Kandi stared down at her hands and shivered violently. She whimpered.

Anne rushed over and knelt beside her. Goading Kandi to move back from the pile, Anne knelt next to her and helped her scoot back. As she stood and brushed off the damp knees of her pants, Anne's foot slipped. She stumbled. *Ralph needs to stabilize this compost area.*

What am I thinking? He will never fix anything again.

With a quick glance at Kandi, Anne ran back to her house. She grabbed her cell phone. Shakily, she punched in 9-1-1.

A woman answered. "Sheriff's office. What is your emergency?"

"I want to report a—" *A what, an accident? A–no, it can't be—a murder?*

"Hello. Ma'am. What's your name?" The voice crisp and concise.

"Anne. I'm Anne." *It's so cold.*

"Okay, Anne. Where are you calling from?"

"From my phone." Anne's hand shook.

"Ma'am, I understand you are calling from a phone. *Where* are you?"

Why is the room spinning?

"Ma'am? Hello—Anne. Are you still there?"

"Yes. I don't… I don't feel very well." Anne struggled to concentrate. Bile rose in her throat.

"Are you standing?" The woman's voice sounded like it was in a tunnel.

"Yes." Anne wiped at her brow, now clammy to the touch.

"Please sit down now, and put your head between your legs. But *do not* hang up. Understand?"

"Yes." Anne sat down just as her legs gave way. She bent over and tried to take deep breaths.

"Ma'am—Anne? Are you there? Can you put your phone on speaker?"

Anne nodded. "Done."

"Anne, now can you tell me where you are located?"

"I'm in the kitchen. I mean, 470 Drury Lane." She tried to focus.

"Good. Now can you tell me what the problem is?"

"Ralph's dead." Anne's voice was quiet.

"And who is Ralph?" the woman asked in a crisp voice.

"My neighbor. Mr. Rogers." Anne's voice caught as she spoke.

Silence on the other end.

She thinks I'm kidding.

Angrily, Anne spat out "This isn't a joke. My neighbor, Ralph Rogers, is dead!" She broke down crying.

"Ma'am, it's going to be okay. We have officers on their way. Just stay in your—"

"Oh, no. Kandi!" Anne shook herself back to attention. Her heart raced.

"Ma'am? Hello, hello? Stay with me, Anne."

Anne didn't answer. Grabbing the phone, she shot out of the back door, yelling, "Kandi, I'm coming!" She sprinted across the yard and past the bushes.

Kandi was still on her knees, clutching her arms tightly to herself, rocking back and forth. The blood on her hands smeared her shirt sleeves. Kandi's teeth chattered, and her lips looked bluish. "You left me! How could you do that to me again?" Tears rolled down her cheeks.

She's going into shock.

Anne dropped the phone into her sweater pocket. She came around behind Kandi and pulled her into an embrace. "It's okay. I'm here now. Help's coming," she whispered. She smoothed Kandi's hair off her forehead and intoned, "its okay, its okay," as she rocked the young woman.

Sirens called from the distance.

"Help's coming. We're okay." Soon she heard the squealing of tires on gravel and people scrambling around her yard.

She turned her head and bellowed, "We're over here!"

A man in a blue uniform rounded the clump of bushes. Kandi turned and buried her face against Anne, seeking refuge as a chick does with a mother hen.

Men and women in uniforms rushed toward them. Two of them eased Anne away from Kandi. They led her toward a stand of aspens. Others bent over Ralph, checking for signs of life.

Trying to focus her jumbled thoughts, Anne welcomed a soft blanket being placed over her shoulders. At the same time, someone spoke to her from a deep well. Even with the blanket, she felt so, so cold. Dizzy.

Out of the corner of her eye, she thought she could see Hope. *Why is she here? Was that fear on her face? What would Hope be afraid of? Am I imagining things?*

A man spoke. "Call it. Time of death—seven twenty-five a.m."

Kandi's scream punctured the air.

The world turned black.

Anne awoke to a flash of light in front of her eyes. She blinked and moved her head, which brought back the dizziness. *What happened?* She tried to sit up.

"Nope, not yet," a man chided. "You've had a shock. You fainted, but you're okay. You're going to be fine. Just lie there for a little while longer."

Anne opened her eyes and spied a man beside her. As her gaze dropped, she saw a masculine hand wrapped around her own. He squeezed her hand with a light reassurance. She moved her gaze upward until her eyes rested on the man's face. Light brown stubble covered the lower part of his face, but it failed to hide the dimple that grew more pronounced as his smile widened.

Where am I? What's going on? She blinked, trying to clear her mind.

Her leaden eyelids refused to stay open. She blinked again. Giving up the fight, she closed her eyes, only to have someone shake her arm.

"Stop." She pulled away from the hand. "Tired. Sleep."

"Sorry, no sleep for you for a bit." The man cajoled in a soothing voice, "I bet you're hungry. Doesn't some breakfast sound good?"

Anne heard the distinctive rip of a blood pressure cuff being pulled off her arm.

"Go 'way." She tried to jerk her hand free.

"No can do. Can you tell me your name?"

"Anne Freemont."

"Okay, Ms. Freemont. Can you tell me the day?"

"Today."

"Yes. It's today. But what day is it?"

Anne rolled her eyes upward, as if the elusive day could be found there, sitting atop her head. "The twelfth?"

"Okay." She heard a soft, suppressed chuckle. "I meant the day, not the date, but that works too. I think you're going to be fine. Do you want to try and sit up now?"

Anne nodded.

Guiding hands supported her until she was upright. Strong arms bore the weight of her back and she leaned heavily on them. The man smelled like buttered popcorn. She took in a deep breath. "Yum. Tasty snack."

Another soft chuckle tickled her ear, then she heard him say under his breath, "Thanks for the compliment."

What the heck is he talking about? Popcorn really sounds good.

"Can I have some?" She might feel better if she ate something salty.

"Some what, ma'am?" a woman interjected. As she moved from her position, Anne could see the woman's face, serious and intent. "Do you want us to transport you to the hospital for evaluation?"

Anne tried again to clear her mind of the lingering fog. "No. I don't need a hospital. I just want to sit, I mean, stand up."

The man and woman, dressed in identical dark blue EMT uniforms, helped her up. As Anne struggled to stand, her legs moved like those of a newborn filly finding its balance for the first time. Swaying for a moment, she held her ground. The morning's events returned with a vengeance.

She swiveled around, taking in the scene. To her left, crime specialists were working within the taped-off compost area while the sheriff's department talked to onlookers: a few local reporters, some of the neighbors. But something—no, someone—was missing.

"Kandi! Where's Kandi?" A renewed energy coursed through her. She wrestled away from the strong arms.

"Ms. Freeman, we'll need to ask you some questions." A man had appeared on her right. He opened a wallet to show his official identification. Bradley Everett. Carolan Springs Police Department.

"Not until I find Kandi. Where's Kandi? She's about

this tall, bright red hair…" Anne's arm moved awkwardly as she stumbled backward. The EMTs caught her arms again and led her to a gurney parked nearby.

A uniformed officer spoke, "Kandi Jenkins has been taken in for evaluation and questioning."

After Anne's refusal to be taken to the hospital, the woman EMT had escorted her back to her kitchen. The warmth of the room enveloped her and chased away the chill of the morning.

The other EMT—Popcorn-man—brewed a fresh pot of bitter, strong coffee, which made Anne grimace, but its heat warmed and revived her. The police detective sat across from her at the scrubbed butcher-block table, and an officer stood sentinel by the door.

The detective pulled a notepad from his pocket. "You ready to answer some questions, Ms. Freemont?"

"Do I need a lawyer?"

"That's for you to decide." Detective Everett clicked his pen.

"No more lawyers," Anne murmured.

"What?"

"No. I'm fine. Thanks."

"Okay, I just need you to tell me everything you can remember from this morning, before you fainted and hit your head."

"I hit my head?" Anne reached up and felt the back of her head. She grimaced.

"Yes, you did," Popcorn-man replied.

The investigator shot him a keep-your-mouth-shut glance. Detective Everett continued. "Let's start with some basics. How long have you lived in Carolan Springs?"

"Just about a month." Anne scooted back in her chair. She started to wrap her arms around herself but thought better of it. Her stained hands rested on the table and she realized with a shudder that it must be blood. She struggled with the urge to vomit.

"Were you friendly with Ralph Rogers?"

"I only met him once." Anne wrapped her hands around the still-warm mug which helped calm her nerves.

Everett looked up from his notepad. "When was that?"

"The day after I moved in."

"Not since?" He stared at her.

"I've been busy with unpacking and trying to get things in place with contractors." Anne felt a twinge of guilt. "I mean we waved and said hi when we got the mail, but that was about it."

"Okay. So back to the day you met him. He came over here, or you went to his house?"

"I went there when I heard Kandi scream—" Anne caught herself.

The room became silent. She felt trapped in their gaze.

Anne took a deep swallow of the coffee to consider her response. *What were you thinking? You can't say you found Kandi and Ralph fighting with her hands grasping an axe.*

"You were saying you heard a scream?" He urged her to respond.

Detective Everett sat silently, waiting for her to continue. Pen poised.

"She wanted to get her chicken back in its run, before it got to Ralph's garden. No big deal, really."

"Oh, okay." His tone of voice relayed that the incident most likely bore no importance.

"Was there any animosity between Ms. Jenkins and Mr. Rogers?"

Anne took another long drag on her coffee. *Kandi seems like a nice kid. No way did she kill Ralph over a dumb chicken. But you were fooled once before.*

Anne's need to reply was delayed by an officer coming up the back porch stairs. Everett got up and went to the door. The officer followed him outside, shutting the door behind him. Words drifted in through the open kitchen window.

Anne strained to hear the conversation. Thankfully, Popcorn-man had followed them, so he couldn't distract her.

"We believe we found the weapon used to kill—"

Everett interrupted him and said something she couldn't make out.

The newcomer continued, his voice quieter, but Anne still caught some of his words—*bloody axe, tossed in bushes, Jenkins.*

Everett reentered the room followed by the others and sat down.

A crime scene investigator arrived. "Brad, you might want to see this." Between latex-gloved fingers, he held a pink piece of paper in an evidence bag. The officer took it from the CSI and handed it to the detective. "We discovered it by the lilac bushes, along with some other papers."

"Do you recognize this, Ms. Freemont?" He held it out for her inspection.

"Ahhh, ummm, it's to me." Anne recognized Kandi's note.

She tried to make light of it. "It must have blown there when my recycling tipped over. I'll make sure it doesn't happen again. A pass on any littering fine, okay?"

She smiled coyly and reached out to secure the note. The note she knew bore the childish scribble and simple reminder of a warm neighborly welcome. That kindness eclipsed by what Anne also recalled had been written in jest—'I could just kill him.'

"It's evidence." The CSI went back outside, taking the note with him.

No. It can't be. Kandi wouldn't kill Ralph. Why would she do it? It makes no sense. Her motive couldn't be a chicken. Though people have killed for much less, sometimes for no reason whatsoever. Had she? Maybe in a fit of anger? Or an accident? No, not Kandi. This doesn't make sense.

Everett interrupted her thoughts. "Anything more you want to tell me about Kandi or the chicken getting into Mr. Rogers's garden?"

Anne needed to buy some time to think. She grabbed the edge of the table, swaying in her seat, as she let out a high-pitched, "Whoa, dizzy..." Keeping one hand on the table, she moved her right hand to her forehead, closing her eyes.

"Brad, I told you to wait and question her later. She took a pretty good knock to the head." Popcorn-man must have returned.

"Okay." Detective Everett shut his notepad and rose from his chair. "Here's my card, Ms. Freemont. We're the assisting organization for this area. You're technically part of the county versus the city. So the Sheriff will be finalizing this investigation."

Anne mumbled, "Okay," and kept up the undulating motion, even though the swaying made her dizzy for real.

As soon as the officers left, Popcorn-man sat down and said, "You can quit the acting now."

Anne regarded him with a 'whatever do you mean' look.

"I...I—" She stopped moving.

"Don't try to con me. I know what's real and what isn't."

She blushed at being caught out. *So much for an acting career.* "Okay, you got me—"

"Sam. I'm Sam Powers."

"Listen, Sam. My thoughts were all jumbled. I didn't want to say anything that could be misconstrued."

"I get it." He pulled the cap from his head, brushed back his brown wavy hair, and put the hat back on with a deft movement. Reaching behind him, he pulled out papers from a backpack he'd slung over the chair.

"Here are instructions for the next twenty-four hours. If any of the symptoms on this list occur, then you'll need to give us a call. Since we're a small town, we're basically your emergency room team. No hospital here. Since you refused additional treatment, you do need to go see your doctor tomorrow, just to get checked over. Who's your doctor?"

"I don't have one yet. I haven't been in town long. The only person that has seen me is Hope." Anne initialed the paperwork he set before her.

Sam took the paperwork and handed her a copy. "She's great. You can go to her. She's an M.D. as well as a naturopath. We're lucky to have her. Best of both worlds—natural and allopathic medicine combined. Anyway, she'll make sure you're good to go. Well, I'm off."

He scratched at the stubble of the day's beard. "See you round, but hopefully not back on the ground."

"Oh, a real comedian. Ha-ha."

He grinned, tipped his cap, and left.

Chapter Four

After the initial shock of Ralph's death, things calmed down for a few weeks. Then reports were leaked to the press. Ralph had sustained trauma to his mid-section, most likely caused by a sharp instrument, but the official cause of death had been blood loss.

Anne took a deep breath, reliving the moment when she'd heard about the medical examiners verdict of homicide. The evidence appeared strong against Kandi. An axe found in her yard fit the wound. Worst of all, Kandi's DNA was found on the axe handle, on Ralph's clothing, and at the crime scene. Other than Ralph's fingerprints, Kandi's were the only ones found on the axe. Coupled with the note about killing Ralph, it had only been a matter of time before Kandi had been arrested on suspicion of murder.

For Anne, seeing the sweet and kind-hearted Kandi being taken away in handcuffs had been devastating. It seemed like a bad dream where you can't wake up.

After Kandi had been arrested and booked, she'd placed a call to Anne from jail. With a heartbreaking, desperation in her voice, Kandi begged Anne to come visit her. Reluctantly, Anne had agreed and the day had arrived.

Anne didn't know what to expect as she walked into the city's detention center. The walls were painted in the latest cast-off colors of the local hardware store. She entered to see a thick glass window with a speaker mounted in it.

To its left, there was an imposing metal door with a guard looking through its small window. A row of plastic chairs sat along one wall, and a pot filled with coffee of doubtful provenance sat on a cart. Some news story played on the television screen mounted in the far corner, the muted sound like that of an incessantly buzzing insect.

Two people hovered at the coffee cart. The woman poured fake creamer out of a bent cardboard container into a cup. Next to her, a young man in his early teens looked up as Anne passed. The woman, most likely the boy's grandmother, responded to his request for the sugar. "You'll be lucky if I don't give you some real lumps. I'm so fed up…"

Anne quick-stepped past the pair to the window. A solidly built woman, her hair pulled back tightly into a bun, strode to the window.

Anne smiled.

The woman didn't. "Yes?"

"I'm here to see Kandi Jenkins."

"Name?" The woman glared at her.

"Anne Freemont."

The woman pulled a clipboard off the wall above the

desk and scanned the list using her finger. "Okay. Take a seat."

While Anne waited, she reflected on how much her life had become entwined with Kandi's. Before Ralphs' murder and Kandi had been arrested, it had become almost a daily ritual for the young woman to show up for a quick chat over coffee in the morning or a cup of tea in the afternoon. Kandi had rapidly won Anne over with her sweet nature, despite their age gap. The two would share meaningless conversation about the weather or some antic of Kandi's chickens and they'd also discussed the strange disappearance of Rusty, who'd gone missing. Kandi blamed it on a mountain lion, but Anne said maybe Rusty had gone on the lam after killing Ralph. They'd laughed at the time but the reality of Kandi's position now made Anne rethink all of their conversations since Ralph's traumatic death.

Yet, while their friendship grew deeper and stronger, they rarely talked about themselves or their pasts. The one thing Anne did know about Kandi was that her husband spent much of his time away for business—a lot of time.

As they'd talked about Ralph. Kandi had remained positive that his murder would soon be solved. But in the back of her mind, Anne remembered all the collected evidence and worried for her new young friend. Had it all been a ruse? Was Kandi capable of murder?

"Anne Freemont, step to the door." The commanding voice broke her reverie.

Anne did as instructed. A tall, burly officer came

and stood at the entrance, giving Anne a glance-over. A buzzer sounded, and the door swung open.

"Remove your jacket, empty your pockets, and put your purse over on the table for inspection." He held up a bag she'd set down next to her purse. "What's this?"

"It's some items for Kandi—Mrs. Jenkins. Is that okay?" The guard took a quick look into the bag, which held toiletries and other personal items.

"We'll go through it and then see she gets it." The guard set it aside on another counter. He took her purse, looked through it, and gave her a nod toward a row of lockers. After she'd put her purse in the locker and he'd secured it, he disappeared around the corner.

The female officer from the front window appeared in his absence. She did a swift pat-down of Anne, who obediently followed orders to hold her arms out to her sides. After a scan with a metal-detector wand, she led Anne toward a small room off the hallway.

Inside, Kandi sat at a table, picking at her cuticles. She wore an orange jumpsuit and cheap flip-flops. Anne's heart clenched.

The female guard stepped to the side.

Kandi looked up as Anne entered the room. Her eyes pooled with tears that slid silently down her cheeks. "Thank you for coming. Jeff's at an important conference for business. He's working on getting a flight back as soon as possible. He'll post bond for me soon so I can get out of here. They wouldn't let me out on my own recogna—" She struggled to finish the word.

"Recognizance" Anne interjected.

Kandi nodded then shivered.

Anne wanted to give her a comforting hug but the guard's warning glance stopped her so she sat down across the metal table from Kandi. She cringed to see the girl wore handcuffs.

"I didn't do it." Kandi moaned, as tears rolled down her face. "Why do they think I would kill Ralph? I have no idea how that axe got in my yard." She took a deep breath and sat up straighter. "You've got to help me. Clear my name. I didn't do this."

"What do you expect me to do Kandi? I'm not a lawyer."

"I have a lawyer. He's driving over from Denver today. I need a detective."

"Okay. Good to know. But maybe you haven't noticed. I'm not a detective, either."

"But I don't have, *like*, anyone else." As her voice rose in anguish, the guard took a step closer. Kandi got the message and lowered her voice. "I've got to find out what really happened. I can't let them pin this on me. I need you to be my Miss Marple."

Pin this on me? Miss Marple? Anne sighed deeply and shook her head.

"Well you can't be, like, Phyrne Fisher. She's young, racy, and hot-to-trot—"

That's the way to get me to help you kiddo. Call me old and boring. Not!

"—and of course, you can't be Poirot or Holmes, because you're, *like*, not a man."

Anne had heard enough. "You can't be serious! Young lady, you are charged with a grave crime, and you're talking fictional mystery detectives?"

"I'm just saying that, *like*, none of them are real detectives, so you could do it."

"Yeah, well here's the thing, missy. The problem with that is I'm not dating a sheriff, police chief, or other law enforcement officer—so how do you propose I gain any information to solve the crime, Ms. 'come back to the real world' Jenkins?"

"You're new here. All you have to do is, *like*, go to the stores, and you'll hear a lot from people talking. They won't even, *like*, notice you."

"Gee. Thanks." Anne groaned.

"Well, no offense, but you could use, *like*, a new haircut."

Seriously? I'd like to shake some sense into this girl. But Anne quickly saw past the bravado, and the very real, very scared young girl emerged in front of her eyes.

Her heart softened. This wasn't the time for lectures. "Look, sweetie, I'm no detective. I don't know what I can do to help, but I'll do what I can. Okay?"

Kandi sucked in a sob and nodded her head. Tears slid down her cheeks. The guard handed her a box of tissues. As she grabbed the tissues, the metal bracelets clanked loudly.

"Thanks." Kandi wiped her eyes and nose.

"No problem. Time's up, though." The officer pointed at the clock affixed to a far wall.

Anne stood. "Anything you need, you let me know. I brought some magazines, some snacks, and a few things for you, like socks, a toothbrush, and toothpaste."

"That's, *like*, so sweet. Thank you. I need to ask you one more favor. If you don't mind, could you go over and feed the girls? Jeff should be able to close them up tonight. The chicken feed is in the metal trashcan." Under her breath, she said, "I don't want whatever got Rusty to get my other girls."

"Yes, I'll make sure the chickens have food and water."

The officer motioned for her to exit at the open door. On entering the hall, Anne turned and glanced once more at the young woman. Kandi sat slumped over onto the table, tissues pushed to her face, handcuffs hanging on tiny wrists, silent sobs wracking her body.

I don't know how I'm going to do it, but I'm helping that girl.

With that final thought, the door slammed shut behind her.

As soon as she got home, Anne went over to feed the chickens. Rusty, the hen that had caused so much fuss initially, was still nowhere to be seen. Kandi often said how her hens would hang around a large woodpile. She squinted at the woodpile. On the side of one log, some reddish-brown feathers clung to the wood. She strode toward it.

"Can I help you?" A loud voice cut through the air.

Startled, Anne stopped. She turned around.

A tall thin man stood a few yards away, eyes hidden under Ray-Bans.

"You must be Jeff. I'm your new neighbor. Anne." She motioned toward her house. "Kandi asked if I'd stop by and feed the chickens."

"In the woodpile?" He shoved the sunglasses up on his head.

"One's missing. Rusty. I thought maybe she'd been roosting there and got trapped."

"Well, it's not. I think you better leave. I'll take care of things now."

Anne struggled to be polite. "I thought Kandi said you were out of town."

He pushed the sunglasses up on his head. Narrowed eyes focused on her. "I was. I just arrived." He pointed toward the door where carry-on luggage stood on the step.

"As much as you travel, you must have great frequent flier miles." She glanced toward the driveway area. "I don't see your car."

"I often leave my car at the airport and catch a shuttle when it's late. I can sleep in the van." He hesitated, and then clamped his lips shut. Mr. Frosty had returned.

"Good to know for my next trip." As she walked back across the street, she glanced over her shoulder and saw that Jeff had followed her around the side of the house. Anne waved, but he didn't return the gesture. A strong tremor coursed down her spine. She sprinted home.

Safely ensconced in her kitchen, Anne breathed a sigh of relief. *He gives me the creeps. I don't care what most people do here about locking doors.* She thrust the deadbolt into place.

After her nerves calmed down, she laughed at her

imagination. This was too nice a day to be locked up. Plus, she was determined that a man would never make her feel afraid or inferior ever again. She unlatched the lock.

But Kandi was still locked up. Poor, sweet girl. Thoughts crowded Anne's mind and all fought for attention. She had no idea where to even begin to help. Maybe she could talk some sense into the girl. Kandi needed real help, not anything Anne could do. But how to convince Kandi?

Anne walked back out to the porch. She wiped the steps off and sat down, replaying the last few weeks in her mind. Other than waving when they saw each other, Anne hadn't gotten to know Ralph very well, but based on what she did know about him, he didn't seem like the type to have enemies. And she seriously doubted he would have killed Rusty, especially after providing Anne with some of his tomato crop.

You never know. Everyone has enemies. But did someone hate him enough to kill him?

As Anne's mind pondered next steps, she turned her attention to a plot of ground off to the side of the porch. It was so close to the house and full of plants that at one time it might have been a kitchen potager, full of vegetables, herbs, and ornamentals.

It might be just the place for a keyhole garden for herbs and flowers. Pulling herself up by the railing, Anne ambled down the steps to the weedy patch. The desire to awaken the sleeping garden couldn't be stopped. She knelt down and attacked the scrap of ground closest to her.

As the pile of weeds grew, the bare earth became exposed. Anne sunk her hands deeply into the moist damp soil. Pulling free from the soil, she stared at her nails covered in dirt. She raised her hands in the air and shouted aloud, "So there, Duke!"

Laughing at her silly display, she decided to go all out and embrace her connection to the earth. She flipped over and sprawled across the cool grass next to the bed. The sun's rays embraced her, and she allowed its warmth to envelop her. She had just closed her eyes when a shadow passed over her.

"Um. Hello." A man's voice intruded into her solitude.

She squinted up into the sun. Stewart, Ralph's nephew, gazed down at her with a "you're a nutcase" look on his face.

Anne sat up. "I'm cleaning out this bed to get it ready for planting next year."

"Okay. Whatever you say." His tone reiterated the "you're crazy" impression.

Anne thought about her current position. *He must think I'm an idiot or an eccentric. Oh, who cares? Maybe that's what crones do.* She chuckled and struggled to stand.

He held out his hand, which she purposefully ignored.

Upright once more, she shielded her eyes from the sun. "So, how may I help you, Stewart?"

"I knocked on the front door but no answer. I told Sam I'd come by and check to see how you were doing since your fall. So I came around here and saw you, um...in the garden."

"I'm doing just fine." She unconsciously rubbed her

head, too late realizing she'd wiped dirt into her hair. "I'm really sorry about your uncle."

"Thanks. It was such a shock. He's always been grumpy, but he wouldn't have hurt a fly. I don't know why Kandi killed him." Stewart frowned and shook his head.

"What makes you think Kandi killed him?" She dusted off her hands.

"It's pretty simple. They've had words over the years. First time, it happened over some property boundary issues. Then she pruned one of his trees without his permission, and of course, the chickens always mangling his garden. If he said anything about it, she acted like she was the victim and made him out to be the perpetrator."

"I just can't see Kandi doing anything like that. She's been nothing but kind to me."

"Well," he lowered his voice, "she's got the history."

"What does that mean?"

"You know. Her mama."

"No. I don't." Anne waited for him to expound on his statement.

"Well, she'll have to tell you about that." He shoved his hands in his jean pockets.

"On another subject, what will happen to Ralph's place now?" Anne pointed toward the house.

"I guess we'll sell it." He shrugged his shoulders.

"We'll sell?" Her brow furrowed.

"Me and Hope. She's his daughter."

"Hope is Ralph's daughter?" That might explain her presence the day of his death.

"Yep. I'm the only other kin. His sister, my mom,

passed away a few years back. His son was killed in the war, and his wife died from cancer." Stewart kept talking, but more to himself. "Boy, the more you think about it, he had a really tough life, and then—bam!—killed by an axe."

He abruptly stopped talking and stared down at Anne. "Hey, you didn't hear or see anything that morning. Did you?"

"No. I didn't hear anything until Kandi screamed." An involuntary shiver coursed through her at the memory.

"Oh, okay. Well, if you think of something, you'll tell me, won't you?"

"Um, sure." *Um, no.*

"Well, best get going." As he reached her driveway, he turned. "If I were you, I'd make sure I locked my doors. You know what they say about the killer coming back to the scene of the crime." He grinned.

Anne watched Stewart cut across to Ralph's yard. Even though the sun shone brightly, she shivered for the second time. If Stewart stood to inherit, he definitely had motive. She'd just found her first suspect.

Chapter Five

Anne slept fitfully that night. She kept waking, listening intently at every creak and groan as the old house settled. Her imagination had gone into overdrive and caused crazy musings about Stewart's words about the killer returning to the scene of the crime.

Wind whipped around the house, rattling the windows and sliding ghostly whispers through unseen cracks in the walls. She shot up in bed when a flash of thunder rocked the house. Another rainstorm on the way. While she was glad for the moisture, this would delay her work in the garden.

Sleep would be impossible. She pulled her terrycloth robe from the corner chair and shoved her feet into fuzzy slippers. Yawning, she made her way down the short wide hall that led into the kitchen.

The gibbous moon illuminated the room, so she didn't bother to flip on the light switch. She turned on the sink tap to fill her glass. Raising it to her lips, Anne caught a flash of light behind the lilacs. She blinked her eyes. Looked once more. Yes, there it was again. Muted, but definitely what looked like a light flickering over by the compost pile.

Could it be that the moon was reflecting off of a piece of metal or something shiny that shone through the trees? Or had the killer *really* returned to the scene of the crime?

She needed an unobstructed view. If she went out on her porch, she might be able to distinguish what she'd seen. She opened the door, but the wind caught the outer screen, slamming the frame against the wall.

The light flicked off.

Now what? She stood motionless. The last thing she wanted was for someone to see her. She waited for a few minutes that seemed like an eternity and then took a hesitant step forward. She squinted toward Ralph's yard. No light. Menacing, heavy clouds cast shadows as the wind moved on its path.

She debated with herself about what she'd seen, when curiosity won over. Just in case there was actually someone there, she grabbed a hammer from the toolbox at her feet. Anne quietly advanced toward the bushes. She tried to justify her investigation and assure herself she wasn't like the dumb female victims she despised in scary movies.

Just to be sure, every so often, she would pause and listen. Was the person she saw doing the same thing? Advancing toward her? Should she just go back inside? Even with her conscience telling her to stop, she kept moving forward.

As she rounded the corner of the lilac stand, she spied a tall figure dressed all in black running across the yard.

"Hey!" Anne yelled, then stopped. *Are you nuts? That could be the murderer.*

She took a step backward. Her foot found something hard and sharp. A whizzing sound. Before she could react, a knock to the left side of her head sent her sprawling into the compost pile.

Noooo. Not the compost pile again! Don't think about Ralph. Don't think about Ralph. Don't think about, ahhh, the blood. She grimaced as she fought back the desire to wretch. Something had dropped beside her as she'd fallen. Anne tried to calm herself and catch her breath. Her mind raced like a hamster on a wheel. Was the killer still out there?

After what seemed like a horrible eternity, she released the breath she'd been holding. She cautiously scanned the area for any signs of movement. Sensing she was alone, Anne glanced back and forth before finally crawling out of the compost pile. With difficulty, she pulled herself to her feet. She looked down as nausea hit her.

That's when she saw the rake.

Was that what had been used to hit her? But what was a rake doing by the compost pile? The scene had been cleared of any evidence and that included any tools.

No matter what, she *had* seen someone. And that someone could be the killer. She needed to get away from here. Anne jogged across her yard and stumbled as she grabbed the porch banister. Her head throbbed.

Remember making fun of people in horror movies? Stupid, stupid, stupid.

Inside the house, she locked the screen door and slid the deadbolt shut on the main entrance. She chased the shadows from the room by turning on every light she could find. She'd left the flimsy café curtains open on the back windows. Was the killer watching her even now? Deciding on his attack?

With a burst of adrenaline fueling her, she found her phone and called 9-1-1.

"Hello, Ms. Freemont. State your emergency."

"This is, hey, how did you—?"

"What's your emergency?"

"Well, it's not really an emergency."

Silence.

Could she feel disapproval coursing through the phone line?

Anne continued. "It's just, there was someone in Ralph's yard, and I got hit on the head, it could have been the rake, but it could have been the real killer, but the guy in black was running across the yard, so how did they—"

"Ms. Freemont. Please remain calm. We'll have someone over shortly." Anne hung up just as she heard the woman say, "Please stay—"

Anne pulled a kitchen chair over to the farthest corner away from the windows. Could the killer see inside? She ran over and flicked off the switch. Turning off the light only served to make her feel even more vulnerable. She crouched down in the corner of the room, away from peering eyes.

Her gaze moved back and forth, seeking an unknown danger. Her body tensed, coiled to spring into action. She'd dropped the hammer when she'd fallen into the compost pile. She had no weapon. She crawled over to the drawer and grabbed a knife. Instead of bringing comfort, it only made her more anxious. What if the murderer took it away from her and used it on her? Panic sought to overtake her.

A huge knot had formed on her temple. She tenderly felt the bump as another hit of nausea caused her to steady herself. This was silly sitting on the floor. She rose and moving across to the fridge, pulled frozen peas from the freezer. She held the package to her head. The cold snapped her mind clear.

Did I almost catch the killer? But how did I see them running and then get hit? Does this mean Kandi isn't the killer? Could Stewart have run across the yard quick enough to cut back and hit me over the head? What had the killer been looking for in Ralph's yard? He knew the police had already been there. Was there something the police hadn't seen?

Footsteps approaching the kitchen door brought a squeal to her lips. It was Sam. He'd gotten here fast. Relief flooded her.

She unlocked the door.

"Hi. Just heard on the dispatch that you'd—Whoa, what happened to you?"

Her tension released into a torrent of tears. Sam put his arm around her and gently escorted her to a chair. He noticed the frozen pea ice pack she held.

"How'd you get hurt? I thought you called in about seeing a person in Ralph's yard."

He looked at her sternly. "Hey, you didn't do something stupid like go over there?"

He moved closer toward her. She took in a whiff of

that popcorn smell again. Strange that he smelled like that over some manly scent.

"Let me take a look-see at that knot."

She set down the ice pack and the nausea hit her again.

"Sit down," he ordered. "How many times have you've gotten hit in the head?" He looked at the knot. "Just to make sure all is well..." He pulled a penlight from his pocket. "I'm going to do a series of quick tests." He shone the light in her eyes. After some questions that seemed to meet with his approval, he sat back in his chair. "I think you're okay, just going to have a nice bruise with that one. I'm going to prescribe not getting hit in the head again."

Anne tried to respond sarcastically but it was too much effort. She simply put the ice pack back on the lump. "Would you like something to drink while we wait? I've got some coffee, um, some tea—oh wait, no tea, some water." *Hmmm, what would happen if a guy drank an herbal tea to help menopausal symptoms?*

"So what actually happened?"

She gave him an edited version of the events.

After a bit of more scolding for her escapade, he smiled. "Our town normally isn't so thrilling. You may wish for some of this excitement once it goes back to its staid complacency."

"I'm ready. I thought this place was going to be quiet. Not!"

A knock at the back door interrupted further conversation.

A deputy from the sheriff's office stood at the door.

Sam said something to the man, who nodded. He gestured at her to stay put. "I'll be back in a minute." The screen door slammed behind Sam as their shapes faded into the night.

Not one to stay put, Anne got up and watched as the two men walked over to Ralph's yard.

After a bit of seeing nothing, Anne sat back down.

The squeak of the screen door heralded their return. "We found the rake and the hammer." The deputy then took her statement as Sam sat listening. As the two men chatted outside, Anne thought about Sam. Over six foot, closer to six two, hair you wanted to run your hands through and deep blue eyes that drew you in. She hadn't noticed any ring on his finger. *Are you nuts? It wasn't that long ago you were in a horrible relationship. Now you're wondering if he's single?*

Sam pushed open the screen door with his elbow. In one hand he held a brown bottle. In the other, a paper bag. He opened the bottle and held it up. "Grabbed this from my truck. Kvass. This is some of the last of my summer brew. I can't wait until next month to start the next batch with apples. Want to try some?"

After she nodded yes, he poured a small amount into a cup and handed it to her. She took a small sip. It was icy cold. "Wow."

"Good, right? Kvass is a fermented grain drink. When I visited the Ukraine, I fell in love with it. I included some citrus and my own secret ingredient. I'd tell you, but then I'd have to kill you." He grinned. Pouring the brew into another cup, he took a hearty swig.

"You didn't tell Ralph, did you?" Anne regretted the words as soon as they'd left her mouth.

"You know that's a weird thing. I mean Ralph wasn't a favorite of many people, but I can't see anyone wanting to harm him, much less kill him."

Anne barely heard his words. She stared at Sam's clothing. Dark pants. Dark jacket. They could have looked black without any light on them. Come to think of it, Sam had arrived pretty quickly. Her brow furrowed as she contemplated adding another suspect to the list.

"Just to ease your mind, no, he didn't know my secret ingredient."

"Well, that's a relief then." She smiled at him before taking another swig of the sour-sweet brew.

"Feeling better?"

She nodded in the affirmative. But it wasn't for the reason he thought. She simply couldn't picture him killing Ralph, much less anyone. She'd learned to trust her gut and Sam had to be one of the good guys. He was too cute not to be. Of course, that's what they'd said about Ted Bundy and probably Jack the Ripper. What was it Agatha Christie had said? Something along the lines of "Every murderer is probably somebody's old friend."

She shivered involuntarily.

He continued without pausing. "It's the B vitamins. I think you may be a bit deficient, due to all the stress lately. Kvass is somewhat like non-alcoholic beer, soda and a bit like Kombucha. It's really good on a hot day. Very reviving. Which will help you calm your nerves before the sheriff arrives. So you can explain why you were in Ralph's yard in the middle of the night."

"But I just gave my statement."

"Yep. But Sheriff Carson returns from vacation tomorrow. You can bet he'll want to hear it from you again. He's not one to leave things undone. He'll probably be all over the reports on Ralph's death and I'll be talking to him about the coroner's findings."

She wanted to change the subject but was curious about his last statement. "Why would you be giving information on the coroner's report on Ralph's death?" She touched the tender area on her temple. Wincing, she put the cold bag of peas back on it.

"Because I'm the deputy coroner."

"What?" Anne sat back against her chair.

"This is a fairly small town. There's a bunch just like ours all up in these mountains. If the coroner is busy or I'm not needed as an EMT, I can assume the role. This way I make sure the scene isn't destroyed by well-meaning individuals trying to help someone that's hurt. There aren't that many deaths and it's easier if I can assume the role without having to wait for the coroner to come out." He took another swig of the brew.

"Because of my training, I know when the victim is beyond help and how to secure the scene. However, the coroner's usually available. We tend to need more help with accidents so I'm a part-time EMT and a part-time deputy coroner. In other words, I work two full-time jobs!" He laughed. The sound was rich and masculine and reminded Anne of all the great things about men.

"So?" She cut into his laughter.

"So… what?"

"Why are you giving the information to the sheriff about what killed Ralph? Is it confidential?"

"Nothing is confidential if Marla is around."

"Who's Marla?" Anne set the frozen peas on the table.

"The reporter you saw at the scene. Oh, you may not have seen her since we were working on you. But the coroner is the one to release any findings. He's away at a conference."

"I don't remember much." *Except seeing Hope. How did Hope get there so soon? And why did she look so frightened?*

"What do you remember?" he asked casually.

"Basically Kandi screaming. Running over." She took a deep breath. "Seeing Ralph. Blood was all over him. On Kandi. It was awful." Unexpected tears sprang to her eyes and she rubbed her upper arms. "He, he was dead. I called the police and then got back to Kandi. And then, I guess, that's when I fainted."

"Your blood pressure was pretty low. I'm presuming you hadn't eaten yet since it was early morning. And as you said, if you're not used to death, and even if you are, it's a big shock. Not surprising that a woman your age fainted."

A woman my age? Geez.

Anne looked at Sam closer. How old was he? He was probably younger than her but how much younger?

"Oh I forgot this." He picked up the brown bag he had set down in the other kitchen chair.

"Let me guess. Popcorn."

"You psychic?"

"Just a good guess."

"The Boy Scouts have been doing a camp this week. Lots of growing boys to feed and popcorn is a quick, filling snack. Plus we have lots of it right now. We made a lot for the camp and had this left over. Anyway, I'll leave it with you. Good night." He got up, grabbed his jacket off the chair, and strode out the door.

"Night." She stood at the back door and watched as he moved off down the drive.

"A woman your age," she mimicked. As soon as he was out of sight, she pitched the bag toward the trash can. It missed the can.

Oh, geez. Forget that. I love popcorn. She picked the bag off the floor and dug into the perfect combination of butter, salt, and crunchy goodness.

At least she had one person she could confidently cross off her suspect list.

.

Chapter Six

A buzzing sound interrupted her sleep. Anne shoved the pillow over her head.

Too hot. She pushed the pillow back under her head. Punched it. Buzzing again.

Her phone. She'd put it on vibrate during her visit to Kandi. Anne groped toward the nightstand and scooped the phone into her hand.

"Hel…lo?" the word came out garbled. Between her midnight outing, her visit with Sam, answering questions for the deputy, and waking up at every sound thinking the killer had returned, she hadn't gotten much sleep.

"Can you come pick me up?" A girl's childlike voice came over the line.

"Who is this?" She rolled over on her other side and immediately regretted it as her bruised head connected with the mattress. Tears of pain sprang into her eyes. The rake hitting her head was going to hurt for some time.

"Kandi."

"Who?"

"Kandi."

Anne sat up and wiped her eyes. "Oh, Kandi. Sorry, sweetie. I couldn't hear you well. What time is it?"

"Seven-thirty."

She groaned. Could a person get a hangover without doing any drinking? "What's up? Do you need me to bring you something?"

"Jeff got in last night, but he has like, a super-important conference call this morning that he can't reschedule. So I have to wait for him to come get me out. They won't release me unless I'm under someone's custody." The implied request hung in the air.

Geez, what kind of a husband is this guy? Wait a minute. He was here earlier than that. He let Kandi sit in jail for another night? Anne tried to concentrate, but her head throbbed and her body ached.

"It would be, *like*, a big favor—"

"Of course, I'll come get you. I'll be there in half an hour."

"Thanks. You're the best!" The line went dead.

Anne forced herself to sit on the edge of the bed. The chill in the room invigorated her but also brought to mind the encroaching need for heating. A new furnace would need to be a top priority on her contractor list.

Pulling the quilt around her shoulders, she stepped to the window and opened the blinds. Just under her window, Stewart bent over something in the plot she'd dug yesterday. Shocked, she took a step back, but he'd straightened and spotted her. He waved.

Anne strode to the kitchen door, angry at the early intrusion. Stewart already stood on the porch, his cap in his hand.

Anne reluctantly cracked the door. She'd need to add a door chain soon.

"Hey, there. Sorry if I scared you. This morning I turned off my uncle's sprinkler system and realized yours might still be on. So I came over to check. Since it's early, I didn't want to disturb you."

You disturbed me all right. She pulled the quilt tighter, a cocoon from the chill seeping through the doorway. The temperatures must have really dropped overnight.

Stewart gestured at the sky. "It's been looking like snow, so best be prepared. Anyway, I see Harry's tag—he puts the tags on the main source so people in new homes can see they've been flushed out. So you're good to go for the season."

"You didn't need to do that."

"Oh, that's what neighbors are for. Got to keep an eye on you." He winked.

"Thanks." She moved to close the door.

"Just don't want any harm to come to you. Some of these things can cause so many problems."

"Thanks again. Have to go now."

"Okay, well, just one more thing. Did I imagine it or did I see you come over in the yard last night? I've been staying at my uncle's to make sure no vandals or teenage thrill-seekers cause any problems. I'd hate for something to happen to you. Lots of accidents can happen at night, when it's dark." He looked at her.

Is he threatening me?

"Thanks, I'll keep that in mind. Goodbye." She shut the door as she heard him respond in kind.

Anne watched him depart. Then with a firm shove, she locked the door.

Kandi grabbed Anne in a tight hug. "I can't tell you how much it means to me that you came. Poor Jeff. He's, *like*, exhausted. He had to fly into town. He was, *like*, able to get the bail settled over the phone. I don't think he's even slept more than an hour or two. Then he has, *like*, this call this morning. It could mean a big promotion for him. I couldn't let him pass that up. I don't want to be selfish. That's why I said not to worry about me."

Kandi continued her babble as Anne drove the young woman home. "I feel, *like*, so grubby. You were so nice to bring me that care package. I don't know what I would have done." Kandi's voice quivered.

Anne took a fleeting look at the young woman who was desperately trying to hold back tears. "I'm happy to do it. You were a big help to me when I arrived in town. It's the least I can do to return the favor. "

"Glad to hear it. So, *like*, when will we start?"

"Start?"

"You know! Finding the real killer."

Anne sighed deeply. "Kandi, I told you. I'm not a detective. I have no idea where to begin. Plus, I know this may come as a shock to you, but killers kill people. I'm pretty happy being alive."

"How can you be so, *like*, flippant at a time like this?"

"Not to worry, I'm flippant all the time."

Scowling, the young woman crossed her arms firmly across her chest.

"Seriously, Kandi, let the sheriff's office handle it. They know what they're doing."

"Oh, yeah. That's why I, *like*, ended up in jail. They only go by the evidence!"

"Did you just hear what you said? What do you want them to go by?"

"I *didn't* do it!" Her voice rose with every syllable.

"Okay." Anne couldn't continue fighting a losing battle.

"Then you'll help?"

"I don't know how you think we'll solve this. I say leave it to the professionals. However, as long as it doesn't involve breaking and entering, I'm in."

"Oh, okay. I guess we won't have to do that."

Anne shook her head. *What on earth did I just commit to?*

Anne followed Kandi's drive along the curve to the back of the house. As the tires crunched on the gravel, the back door flew open. A tall gangly man appeared.

Oh, yippee. Jeff the Jerk.

A set of noise-cancelling earphones stuck out from his ears like an alien Mickey Mouse hat. He held his smart-phone in his hand. He motioned to Kandi with an abrupt wave, but put a finger to his lips. This must be the conference call.

Kandi vaulting from the car toward him reminded Anne of a puppy that doesn't realize her owner is abusive.

Jeff kept up his conversation. He motioned to Kandi to stop. The young woman stood waiting, her face flushed with embarrassment.

Anne lugged the box of Kandi's things from the backseat. As she approached Kandi, Jeff looked over at Anne. His dismissive look was all too familiar. She knew his type. How could she not? She'd been married to a man just like him.

While Anne assessed Jeff's character, he looked at her with judging eyes. She knew the instant when he had deemed her "unworthy." Jeff turned and faced away from them as he continued speaking to some distant person.

Anne dropped the box at Kandi's feet. She mouthed see you later and motioned her intent to leave. Kandi grabbed Anne's arm and whispered, "Please. It shouldn't be much longer. I'd really like for you to meet Jeff."

Anne's mind and emotions warred. *Should I tell Kandi we've already met?* She'd give him a few minutes. Then she was out of there. Thankfully, Jeff ended the call, putting an end to her internal debate.

Jeff pulled the headphones down around his neck. He clutched the phone with a firm grip.

"Hey, baby." Kandi threw herself into his arms.

He pushed her back. "What the heck, Kan? How in the world do you let yourself get into these messes? Do you know how much it cost me to bail you out? I had to get the lawyer to take money out of your trust. Lucky we did that provision."

Undeterred, Kandi ignored his rebuke. "Honey, I want you to meet Anne. She's moved into the old Straiter place." Kandi motioned in the direction of Anne's house.

Jeff looked at Anne, but he too said nothing of their earlier encounter. "I'm glad someone moved into that house. It needs some fixing up. I know a great designer—"

"I think I can handle it." Anne's retort came out sharp.

"Suit yourself."

"Kandi, I'm leaving. If you need anything, give me a call." Anne strode back to the car and put it in reverse.

As she left, thoughts gathered in her mind. *Jeff had been home the evening I saw someone running from Ralph's yard. He had the same build as the figure I saw that night. But what does that have to do with Ralph's death?*

For Anne to really help Kandi, she had to find out everything she could about Jeff.

"Come in. I'm back here!" Hope's voice carried through the opening.

Anne peeked into the hall. A light shone from a door off to her right. She walked toward it. Inside the room, she found Hope surrounded by bottles full of herbs. In the middle of the table stood a scale that Hope was using to measure out various herbs and off to the side sat a large brown bottle. Another counter held jars filled with various herbs and a clear liquid.

"Oh. Hi. I thought you were Susan. I'm expecting a delivery. I'm making tinctures and I've got a special herb order that should be in today. Hopefully." She crossed her fingers and smiled.

She covered the herbs with a cloth. Snapping off the latex gloves she wore, she dumped them into a bin. "Let's go to my office."

Anne removed her tweed jacket as she followed Hope. Partially hidden behind a screen, a door opened onto the examination room Anne remembered from her first visit. Behind a beautiful antique oak desk, medical degrees covered the wall. Instead of taking a seat behind the desk, Hope plopped down on a large yoga ball. Facing the desk, two comfortable-looking chairs in sage green beckoned. Anne took a seat. Hope scooted over until she was across from Anne.

"What can I help you with today? How's the tea working for you?" Hope folded her hands on the desk.

"Actually, I am feeling much better. Thank you."

"I heard about your accident." At Anne's confusion, Hope replied, "Small town. No secrets here. Everyone knows everyone *and* everything. Look, I recommend that you come in for an appointment. We'll do some tests and keep you a healthy woman. I don't like hearing about you fainting along with all these falls and bruises."

Anne touched the sore spot. "I'll set up an appointment. But that's not really why I'm here."

"Yes?"

"This is going to seem strange, but I don't know anyone else to ask. I thought maybe you could help me."

"Ask away and I'll see if I can help." She adjusted her balance on the ball chair.

"So you know Kandi. Can you tell me a bit more about her earlier life—"

Hope held up her hand like a stop sign. "There's no way she killed Ralph. I don't know what they're thinking by even accusing her."

"Then who?"

"Not a clue. I can't imagine anyone killing Ralph. Except maybe me, of course." Hope laughed, but it fell flat.

"What?" Anne blurted out.

"You probably don't know this, but Ralph is—was—my father."

"Um, well—"

"Yes, long story. But you're here to talk about Kandi. What do you need to know? But first, I could go for a cup of hot tea. You?"

Anne waited until Hope had placed a steaming cup of tea in her hands. She took a sip. "This is nice."

"Chamomile and nettle. Good for nerves and the liver. Plus I added a bit of local honey. I swear that Bill's honey is the best in the area. Anyway, where were we? Oh, yes. You want to know about Kandi. She was still in elementary when I was in high school, so I'll have to think back. If I recall it right, things started going bad when she was maybe, oh, twelve or thirteen. By then, I'd moved away to study medicine up at Bastyr University in Washington. But I remember hearing the rumors when I came back on summer break.

"Her mother just up and took off one day, leaving Kandi and the two boys behind. Abandoned them downtown at the ice cream shop with just enough money for an ice cream sundae. She'd left a note at the house about 'finding herself.'" Hope made quotes with her fingers. "But what she really meant was running off with some rich guy who didn't want her kids."

Hope shook her head, took a sip of tea, and set the cup down on a coaster. Using both hands, she ruffled her cropped hair. "At any rate, the twins—the boys—were, let me see…yes, about sixth graders. They all went to live with her grandfather, but Kandi pretty much ended up raising the boys. Plus she was a housekeeper and cook for the grandfather too. He simply wasn't up to raising kids at his age. You've got to hand it to her—she put in a lot of work every day after school. On the weekends she babysat to help make ends meet, too."

"I thought I heard something about a trust fund?" Anne ventured.

"Oh, yes. That happened, I guess, a little over a year ago. But need to back up a bit. Years go by. Not a word from the mom. For all everyone knows, she's off living the high life, or she's dead. One day a stretch limo pulls up at the grandfather's house. By the way, that's the house Kandi's living in now. She inherited it."

"So Kandi received it after her grandfather—" Anne interjected.

"Well, that's another story. Kandi's brothers moved on but Kandi stayed at home, caring for her grandfather. Then one day when Kandi was away, her grandfather fell off of a ladder and broke his hip. He went to step on an upper rung and it broke beneath him. There were some ugly rumors about what happened but nothing could be proven. It was determined to be a freak accident. He went to a nursing home and died just a few months after that."

"How convenient for Jeff," Anne whispered under her breath.

"I see you're not part of the Jeff fan club." Hope snickered.

Anne's face heated up. "Sorry. I didn't realize I'd said that out loud."

"You don't have to apologize to me. Not a fan of the guy. In fact, he gives me the creeps. I've often thought Jeff may have had something to do with Kandi's grandfather's accident." She took another sip of tea.

Anne thought back to the figure she'd seen. Could it have been Jeff? But why kill Ralph?

"Sorry," Anne said. "Please continue with your story."

Hope nodded. "Turns out Kandi's mom had stage four cancer. She wanted to make it right with the kids before she died. The boys are off backpacking the world, but she finds Kandi. She wants to make amends and spend the last bit of time she has left with her kids. But Kandi doesn't want anything to do with her. Jeff tries to get her to listen. She refuses. Kandi tells her mother to get out and never come back."

Hope cocked her head. "What was her name? Can't remember now. So the mom ended up dying a few months later. She left the three kids huge trust funds. Next year when Kandi turns twenty-five, she'll have full access to hers."

"What are we talking money wise?"

"From what I've heard, millions."

"Millions?" Anne set her cup down on the table. "That's a lot of motive—I mean money."

"Yes. Jeff lucked out by marrying a very-soon-to-be wealthy woman." She looked pointedly at Anne.

"Yes. How lucky for him." An idea occurred to Anne. "So what happens if Kandi is convicted of Ralph's murder?"

"I guess it would stay in trust. I know Kandi told me that Jeff has power of attorney over it should anything happen to her. But who knows? Not sure what happens if she were to be convicted of Ralph's murder." Her mouth tightened. "I'd hate to see that man get one penny."

"Interesting. So when did Jeff and Kandi marry?"

"Let's see. I think it was just after the visit from Kandi's mom. I believe they eloped. No one can say for sure but I'm fairly certain that Jeff talked with Kandi's mother. He can put on the charm when he needs it. So he knew Kandi would be coming into money."

Anne looked down at the dregs of tea leaves in her cup. If only they could give her the insight to see into the future. One thing she did know. Jeff wasn't a nice man, and she would bet her last dollar that he married Kandi to get to the millions in her trust fund. But would he go as far as murder?

Could Jeff have said he was out of town, flown into the city, and driven in that night? He could have killed Ralph, thrown the axe in the bushes of their home, and headed back to his conference. He could simply say he'd been asleep all night. The next day he could act like he'd been at the conference all morning. Then he could have flown back out to be at Kandi's side and play the role of doting husband. Unfortunately, he'd failed that part big time.

Kandi did need help, but maybe her enemy was closer than either of them had considered. She needed to get with Kandi and figure out the situation with Jeff.

"Well, I'll let you get back to work. Thanks for the tea and the information. By the way, it's none of my business but I happened to notice Kandi's tattoo."

"Oh yes—*Past*—right?"

Anne nodded.

Hope stood up. "Well, as you can imagine, the strain of her mother leaving and then dying with no reconciliation along with losing her grandfather took its toll. I recommended Kandi seek out some therapy. She did and when she completed it, she got the tattoo. She says it reminds her that the past is behind her. Now she can look forward." She shook her head. "I hope for Kandi's sake they can figure out what really happened."

"Me too. She's such a sweet girl." Anne grabbed the tweed jacket off the chair. "This weather is sure nippy in the mornings and evenings now."

"Yes, it's that time of the year when you really need to layer all the time because you just don't know what to expect weather-wise. As we always say in Colorado, wait five minutes if you don't like the current weather."

Anne crossed the room. As she reached the door, she turned. "Just one more thing. You said something about you killing Ralph?"

Hope laughed. "That's another story for another time. But I certainly wouldn't have killed him with an axe. I'd have poisoned him."

Chapter Seven

Anne waved goodbye to Hope, who had risen from her perch, and then exited the office.

Reminder to self, no more tea with Hope. She chuckled. She heard the back door open and rounded the corner to encounter Eliza headed down the hallway. Seeing Anne, the woman stopped abruptly. Her eyes widened. *She must be trying to remember where she knows me.* Anne smiled. "Hello. Good to see you again."

"Again?" Distress marred Eliza's face for a split second.

"You know. Someone had hit your bumper."

"Oh yes, quite. I apologize for my manners that day. I was in such a state over someone doing such a horrible thing." She hesitated. "But I guess we never fully understand what a person is going through at that moment. Do we?"

"True. They probably didn't even realize they had hit your car."

"Exactly." Tension seemed to leave her as she spoke. "However, I do know who it is, um, was."

"Oh that's good. You can get their insurance to pay for the damage."

"I don't think so." Eliza removed one of her purple kid gloves.

"Why not?"

"It was Ralph Rogers."

Anne gulped. This town really was interconnected.

"Here's the valerian tincture." Hope's voice carried as she appeared around the corner. "Oh, sorry. Didn't know you were still here, Anne."

"Just leaving. Thanks again for the tea and the conversation." She exited the back door and walked home on a recently discovered shortcut that cut off quite a bit of time if she wanted to walk to town. Anne's thoughts swirled along with the leaves dancing in the wind.

Could Hope be the murderer? If she'd killed Ralph, why do it now? What could be the motive? Technically, she could have used an untraceable poison to disable him and then killed him with the axe. No, it made no sense. From all accounts it didn't seem like a planned attack.

Anne sighed deeply. She puffed out her cheeks as she exhaled her frustration. *How do fictional detectives figure it out? They don't have all the evidence either. Just as I think I've got it narrowed down, another person with a motive pops up. Why did I promise to help Kandi?*

"First things first. We need to make a list of suspects." Kandi pushed the button on her coffeemaker. The young woman looked better after a few nights of sleep in her own bed.

"That's great, Kandi, but please remember I'm new here. I only know a small group in town so my suspect list is pretty small." Wood crackled in the fireplace from a recently started fire. Two cozy rockers stationed in front of the hearth beckoned. Lights glowed from table lamps making the room warm and comforting. Anne shrugged out of her jacket, hanging it on a nearby empty coat tree.

"But that's how you will help!" She came over and hugged Anne before returning to her tasks. "I can't imagine anyone in this town killing Ralph. Since you're new, you will see people in a different light. You know, spot the bad guy."

Yes, but you probably wouldn't want me telling you he's your husband. Anne took a moment to warm her hands in front of the fire.

"I knew we could use help, so I called on some people to contribute to our suspect list."

"Knock, knock." Eliza's voice came from the front.

Kandi clapped her hands. "And here they come, right on time." She yelled out, "Come on back. We're in the kitchen."

Eliza entered. Anne knew she was staring, but couldn't look away. The woman moved like a black panther, sleek and beautiful, mesmerizing with her grace and splendor. In a sea of white faces, this woman was like an exotic foreign creature that had accidently found its way into a barnyard.

But panthers are also very deadly. Could she have killed Ralph? What would have been her motive? Did she snap over Ralph hitting her car? She definitely seems uptight about something.

Eliza finally noticed Anne's stare. She smiled. Her perfect white teeth stood out against the coffee skin and ruby-red lips. "I didn't realize you would be here as well." Eliza removed her cashmere coat and neatly folded it over a side chair. On top of the coat, she carefully placed her fur-trimmed hat. Then she proceeded to take off her cream suede gloves. Unlike most people removing gloves, Eliza delicately pulled one fingertip at a time until the glove lay loose on her fingers. After removing them, she placed the gloves into a pocket inside her stylish Birkin handbag. Eliza now sported a vibrant purple nail polish.

"Kandi asked me to participate. Though not sure what I'll be able to do other than offer moral support."

"Sometimes the support of another is the only way that we are able to survive in this cruel world." Sadness moved across Eliza's face, though she tried to hide it under a false smile. Before she sat down, Eliza reached into her purse and brought out a canvas bag. "Kandi dear, may I use your bathroom? I need to prepare my hands."

"Just go ahead. I don't think you have to go to the bathroom just to put on lotion."

"Here?"

"Sure, go ahead." Kandi continued assembling glasses next to a pitcher of lemonade.

From the bag she carried, Eliza pulled out a piece of felt, wooden toaster tongs, a set of white cotton gloves, and some fleece. Finally, she retrieved what looked like an expensive jar of face cream. Anne watched intently as Eliza liberally laced one of her hands with the creamy mixture. Then with the help of the tongs, she slowly slid the glove over it. When both hands were gloved, she wiped the jar with the fleece and put everything into the little bag. From there she placed it in her purse.

Whatever Eliza does, she is rolling in the bucks. That purse is easily $25,000 or more.

As if on cue, Kandi joined them at the table. "I don't know if you know this, but, *like*, Eliza is a model. Her hands are, *like*, in all types of magazines. Cool, right? Next time you see an advertisement with a celebrity in a magazine, check out her hands. They're probably Eliza's."

"I expect that's very exciting." *Explains the weird hand and glove thing, as well as where the money comes from.*

"Not as much as you would think." Eliza placed her hands in her lap. "Quite a few people in the industry are not very nice. It really is all an act for them."

Anne chimed in. "Don't I know it. People can appear one way in public, but be entirely different in private."

Eliza closed her eyes and took a breath. "Please forgive me. I have started us down a rutted path. However, this is no excuse for my statement."

Kandi broke the tense moment with a laugh. "Seriously? You know what they say—every time you, *like*, point one finger at someone else, you point three others back at yourself. I, for one, can't judge anybody. I'm too busy keeping up with my own faults without looking for them in others!" She gave a light squeeze on

Eliza's shoulder as she returned to the counter. "Now, would you like a cup of coffee? Just brewed it."

"Thank you for asking, sweet Kandi. Might you have anything without caffeine?"

Anne noticed the forced smile. Once Eliza sat down, light from a nearby table revealed that even skillful makeup application couldn't hide bloodshot eyes, dark circles, and puffiness. Eliza was definitely struggling with something.

Kandi raised the coffee carafe with a questioning look and Anne nodded yes to the hot brew. She turned her attention back to Eliza. "Are you not feeling well?"

"I am not sleeping as well as I would like." A deep sigh escaped her lips. "This is why I went to see Hope."

Anne touched the woman's arm. "Please, if you need anything, don't hesitate. Us 'girls' need each other."

"That is very thoughtful. Thank you for your generous offer."

Anne patted her arm. Then reaching out, she grabbed a legal pad Kandi had placed on the table. "Okay, are we ready to get—"

"We're here!" Hope and her mother, Faith, had come in while they'd been talking. "Sorry we're late. I had an appointment that went a bit longer than expected." She guided her mother across the large room.

Hope retrieved a muslin packet from her pocket. Taking a pinch of the herbs from the bag, she placed them in a tea ball Kandi provided. When Hope spied Anne watching, she said, "For clarity." She put the tea in to a cup of water.

Faith hadn't spoken. The elderly woman now stared

off into space. Did her mother have dementia? What a heavy burden on Hope.

"I brought enough herbs in case any of you would like some herbal tea as well. I expect we could definitely use some clarity as we begin." Hope held up the packet in her hand.

"Sounds good to me." Kandi plopped down on the edge of the chair opposite Faith.

Eliza replied, "Yes, please do."

As Hope prepared tea, Anne spoke, "Kandi, I've been meaning to tell you. This is such a cozy room. I love it."

Kandi smiled as she glanced around contentedly. "I've always wanted a gathering place, and I'm always drawn to the kitchen. After my grandfather passed on, the house became mine. I guess Pops knew how much this old place meant to me. Anyway, I begged Jeff to tear down the wall between the old kitchen and the dining room. In the process, we uncovered the old fireplace. Luckily, it was still usable. So we had it updated, and now this room has become, *like*, my favorite place." She began to tear up. "But all this could be taken away from me if I have to, *like*, go to trial, and they convict me of Ralph's murder."

The old woman leaned forward and took Kandi's hands in hers. Faith looked at Kandi through glazed eyes.

Eliza squirmed in her seat. Hope stopped pouring water into the teapot. She went over to Kandi and embraced her. "We're not going to let that happen, not if we can help it." She turned to everyone. "Right?" They all responded in unison, and nodded in agreement.

Kandi sniffled. "Thanks everyone. Now, where should

we start?" She joined them at the table. A bang of the screen door didn't allow for any answer.

"Hey, Kandi, I just came by to—" Stewart entered the room. "What's going on here?"

"They're going to help me figure out who really killed Ralph."

"Well, is that so? Then I'm staying. I want to hear what you all think." He grabbed a chair from the table, flipped it backward, and sat down, his arms hanging over the wooden spindles.

"I suppose, *like*, that's all right. The more help, the better for me."

"Kandi!" Jeff's voice bellowed down from upstairs. Feet pounded down the flight of steps. "Kandi! I told you—" He entered the kitchen carrying a pair of pants. He still wore his dress shirt and tie but these stood in opposition to his gray sweatpants.

Spotting the group, his tone turned sickly sweet. "Honey, can I speak with you for a moment?" He motioned for her to join him. As the couple left the kitchen, Anne moved closer to the passage. When had she gotten so protective of this girl? Oblivious to her, the others chatted with one another while Faith made tea.

Jeff's voice, though low, was still audible. "I thought I asked you not to park in the garage. Look." Anne heard the rustle of fabric. "I stepped in that puddle out there. It stained my pants. It messed up my shoes too."

"Sorry, Jeff. I figured since you're gone so much—"

Anne moved quickly as Jeff marched back through the kitchen and up the back stairs. He didn't stop or acknowledge the group. Kandi returned, carrying the muddied pants. She made a joke about the situation before putting the slacks into a bag. But no quip could take away the flush on the young woman's cheeks.

"Shall we get started?" Hope interjected, ignoring the scene they had just witnessed. She pulled a pad of multicolored sticky notes from her purse.

Anne realized that her entire list of suspects was in front of her. *Is the murderer here? What about Jeff? I almost hope he's the killer so they lock him up and throw away the key.*

Anne listened as the group spouted names of possible suspects. The list grew long. "Seems like Ralph had more enemies than friends."

"Hey! That's my uncle you're talking about." Stewart half rose from his chair.

"Oh, stop it. You didn't like him that much either." Hope balled up a sticky note and threw it at him. "In fact, you're probably the killer."

"Funny, ha-ha. If you weren't a relative …" He grinned at Hope.

"Well," Anne said quietly, "you do have a motive."

He turned to her. "Are you serious?"

She shrugged her shoulders. *Are you nuts? Why did you just say that? Don't you remember how he threatened you about coming to harm?*

Hope jumped into the conversation. "She's right. Any of us in this room could have done it."

Anne fidgeted. *Please, oh, please, let it not be Hope. I'd rather not die from drinking a poisoned tea.*

"Really? Says who?" Stewart snapped.

Hope pulled off a yellow notepaper. She wrote boldly

in black: STEWART. "I think this may help us. For grins, let's start with us. We'll use the yellow post-it for the names, the orange for the motive, the green one for alibi, and so on. What do you all think?"

"Okay. I'm game. Hold on." Kandi jumped up from her seat, and left the room. With her exit, an uncomfortable silence enveloped the group. She returned lugging a large picture frame with a whiteboard in the middle. Stewart hopped up and grabbed the frame from Kandi.

"Let me get that for you." He smiled down at Kandi.

"First, Stewart." Hope posted the yellow paper to the frame. "So where were you from eight that evening until around six the next morning?"

"Why that time frame?" Anne inquired.

"Ralph left the diner around seven-thirtyish the evening before his death. By the time he got home, and then went out to his backyard, we're talking at least eight at night. Kandi found his body around six the next morning." Hope reached over and comforted Kandi who had tensed at the recollection.

Eliza shivered. "It's just too horrible."

"Come sit by me, dear." Everyone jumped as the older woman spoke for the first time. "You need not be afraid any longer. They can't find you here." Faith looked directly at Eliza, whose shocked face contrasted greatly with her usual calm demeanor.

Hope rose and went over to her mother. "Mama, here. Let me put this over you." She tucked a nearby throw around the woman and rejoined the group sitting around the antique oak table. She lowered her voice and spoke to Anne. "Some days are good and some not so good. We just never know from day to day."

"What did Faith mean by what she said to Eliza?" Anne poured more coffee into her mug.

"She's, *like*, got the sight," Kandi quipped to Anne.

"What?"

"Oh, yeah. She, *like*, got it from her mama, and, *like*, her mama's mama had it too. Some in town say it's the gift of second sight. The old-timers call it witchcraft."

"Does she have it?" Anne nodded toward Hope.

"If she does, she keeps it hidden. She's pretty good at knowing what's wrong with a person though." With Hope correctly diagnosing her menopausal symptoms, Anne couldn't dispute that. Blood tests advised by Hope had also shown Anne was a bit anemic and had some adrenal insufficiency caused by stress. Hope's medicinal protocol had helped Anne immensely and she was already feeling much better.

Hope spoke to the group. "Let's see, where were we? Oh yes. A killer. Back to you then, Stewart. You never said. Where were you?"

"I wasn't even in town that day. I was over in Frisco with a delivery. I got sleepy driving home, so I pulled over into a parking lot and slept in my truck."

"So no one can vouch for you or your whereabouts that evening?"

"No. But why would I want to kill the old man? He's always been good to me. He got me set up with my van and helped me get my business going."

"What about the house and property?" Anne interjected. "You stand to inherit it."

He looked at Anne. "Hope and I both inherit. Anyway, what do I want with that old place?"

"You could sell it," Anne answered. "Ralph's lot is definitely bigger than mine and Kandi's. Or he could have left you money in his will. Maybe he told you that recently, and you thought you could use the money now versus later. We saw you storming off from his place, mad about something."

Stewart gaped at Anne. "You've been thinking a whole lot about this, haven't you?"

"Not really. I'm simply saying you have motive."

"Well, how about this? All of us have been here for years. Yet you show up and within a month, my uncle is dead. You just said his property is better than yours. You got hurt in his compost pile. Maybe you decided to retaliate, but it went too far. And just after I said the killer returns to the scene of the crime, I see you out in the middle of the night in my uncle's yard!"

Anne felt the intense stares. One person's gaze in particular.

Kandi's.

Chapter Eight

The meeting at Kandi's had lasted over two hours, but they had come up with nothing conclusive. Anne wanted to talk to Kandi about getting some real professional help. Anne decided to take it up with her the next time they met.

As luck would have it, they met up a few days later. After Kandi had grabbed some juice from Anne's refrigerator, Anne spoke. "Um, so tell me a bit about—"

You, *like*, hate men." Kandi pointed her finger at Anne.

"I don't '*like*' hate men. Plus that makes absolutely no sense. How can you like hate men?" Anne grabbed at Kandi's finger. "Don't be pointing that at me. It has a nail in it."

"What?" Kandi cocked her head. With her hair pulled up into pigtails she looked a bit like a cocker spaniel puppy, one with bright red fur.

"Oh, forget it. But just to settle it so we can move on, I don't hate men."

"Yes, you do!"

"No. I. Don't!" Anne took a deep breath. She knew

Kandi was teasing, but her emotions concerning men still felt a bit raw. "First, I don't know how we even got on this subject to begin with. Second, I have no idea where you got the impression that I hate men."

"Well, you have warned me off about Stewart since you think he could have, *like*, the best motive for killing his uncle. I can tell you're, *like*, not a fan of Jeff. Every time he comes into the room you act like you've just smelt something bad. You, *like*, just told me this morning how rude Sheriff Carson is. Need I go on?"

Anne felt she was battling a twelve-year-old.

"You know, *like*, Stewart stands to make quite a bit of money. *Like*, off his uncle's house. I'm not, *like*, going to talk about Jeff. And Carson, *like*, was rude, *like*." Anne grinned widely at Kandi.

"I don't know why you're getting so, *like*—"

"Argghhh. If you say *like* one more time, I'm going to bang you over the head!" She dug through her recycle bin and threatened Kandi with an empty paper towel tube.

"Why do you, *like*, have a problem with...oh." Kandi giggled. "I didn't even know I was saying it."

"Well, you are. A lot. I'm glad your placeholder is the word 'like' versus a cuss word, though."

"Okay. I will, *like*—" She covered her mouth and giggled. "I will try not to say like." She curtseyed. "Ma-lady." Kandi crossed her arms. "Hey—you're getting off topic. I still say you hate men!"

"I'm not going to argue with you. I like men."

"Good." Kandi picked up her phone, typed in a text message, and pressed send. Her phone pinged with a return message. "You need to be at the Plowman's Pub at seven tonight. They do a mean chicken-fried steak. Your date will be wearing a red tie."

"What! Did you just set me up? I don't want to go on a blind date!"

"I thought, *like*—" She stopped, then started again. "I thought you didn't hate men?"

"I don't. I'm simply not ready to date." Anne slumped back in her chair.

"You don't have to get married. Go have some fun. You never leave your house."

A knock at the front door interrupted the tirade. Kandi jumped up and Anne strode to the door, opening it.

Kandi continued her chattering, "Now what are you going to wear?"

"Wear?" Eliza stood at the door.

"Eliza. Come in. Perfect timing." Kandi motioned the woman to join them. "Would you like some tea?"

"I wanted to bring you some flowers Kandi. I feel so horrible about…" The thought trailed off, and Anne watched as a somber expression passed across Eliza's face. "Anyway, Jeff told me you were over at Anne's. I hope I'm not intruding."

Kandi moved quickly and embraced the woman, who stood a good head taller than her. "That's so sweet. Thank you."

"So what is this I hear about something to wear?" Eliza handed the flowers to Kandi.

"Anne has a dinner date tonight." Kandi grinned smugly.

"Oh, how fun." Anne felt Eliza giving her the once-over. "What *are* you going to wear?"

Anne's thoughts traveled back in time to when she had a closet full of couture. She'd donated them to a thrift store that supported battered women.

That had been when she knew she'd truly left her old life—and Duke—behind. He couldn't force her to be or do anything she didn't want to be any more. She was free.

"Hello? Anne? Daydreaming?" Kandi's voice chased away the past.

Anne glanced up to see Eliza and Kandi staring at her.

"Looked more like a nightmare." Eliza frowned.

Anne ignored the pair. "I don't have anything to wear. Basically a few pairs of jeans, some tops, and the dress you saw me in the other day. Oh well, that's unfortunate. But looks like you'll just need to call him back and cancel."

Kandi shook her head. "Oh no, you don't. That's the dumbest excuse ever. You're going, even if you wear what you're wearing now!"

"Oh. This will not do." Eliza sized Anne up. "What are you a ten to twelve?"

Anne shrugged.

"Wait here. Kandi, can you help me get some clothes out of my vehicle?" Eliza exited the house, with Kandi trailing behind her.

Returning quickly, Kandi held the door while Eliza entered the room, a pile of dresses on hangers draped over her arms. "Yes, I think one of these will do. Stand up, please."

Anne obeyed. Eliza moved quickly, sizing up the dresses, throwing those she rejected over the back of a chair, until she came to a flowing shift of mint green with a matching jacket. "This." She held it up in front of Anne.

Kandi gasped. "Beautiful. Where did you get these?"

"Designers often do knockoffs and samples. I take whatever the other models don't want and give them to a charity I support. Go try it on."

"Wow. That's like awesome timing." Kandi beamed while Anne went into the bathroom to try on the dress. She gazed at herself for a long moment in the full-length mirror attached to the wall. The dress fit like a glove. She fingered the material on the jacket. The tag showed a size ten.

Duke would have thrown a fit. It would have been just like that time before that fundraiser when he'd shamed her into a ridiculous amount of dieting so she could look appropriately skinny on his arm. She'd landed in the hospital after that one. She'd much rather be a size ten than do that again.

Even after gorging herself on food and drink after she'd left Duke, Anne knew she was still an attractive woman. She didn't need to be bone thin to feel good in her own skin. She smiled. It had been a while since she'd felt this good about herself.

Kandi and Eliza clapped as Anne returned to the kitchen and took a turn around the area. They all laughed as she did her worst catwalk imitation, striking poses and making duck faces over her shoulder.

Eliza looked at Anne and then turned to Kandi. In unison, they cried, "Marilyn!"

"Who's Marilyn?" Anne removed the jacket and placed it back on a hanger.

"She's the genius who's going to do something super cool with your hair. Go change and let's get moving. No time to waste." Kandi reached for her phone.

The day passed quickly. Marilyn hennaed Anne's hair into a glossy auburn color, which she then cut and styled to enhance Anne's naturally flowing curls. Gone forever was the straightened bleached blond. Or its unkempt opposite of dull brown strands. After that, the star treatment had continued with a manicure and pedicure. She'd forgotten how nice it felt to be preened over. The transformation complete, Anne stood in her kitchen, and was inspected by her fashion entourage.

"Whoa. You look amazing." Kandi cheered.

"Beautiful." Eliza air-kissed each of Anne's softly blushing cheeks.

While Anne had been changing, Kandi had also gone home and changed her own outfit. Anne glimpsed Kandi absently pushed something red down into her pocket.

Kandi smiled at Anne. "Listen, I have to go into town for some errands. Is it okay if I drop you off? And not to worry, I'll be back in a jiff in case you want to skip out early. I have one small errand I have to do before they close. Then I'll be right back with you. "

Anne gulped. Her stomach clenched. Reality came plunging back in. Now she had to go meet a man. A man she didn't want to meet. She knew that few men were like Duke, but she couldn't help the dread that enveloped her.

"I haven't been out on a date in a very long time. I'm not sure I'm ready for this. Maybe it would be okay to cancel for today and reschedule?" Anne pleaded with Kandi.

"Don't worry. It will be fun. In fact, I'll make you a wager that by the end of the evening, you'll be thanking me. So trust me, okay?" The young woman's face lit with delight.

"Okay. Yes, that would be nice. Thanks for everything. You're so sweet. Really. Sorry I've been such a pest lately." They went out and got into Kandi's truck, which had been cleaned.

"No worries. Hope told me to give you some grace due to the menopause thing."

Great. I'm old again.

"Oh, that reminds me. Here." Kandi handed Anne a tiny brown bottle. "This is from Hope."

Anne uncapped the bottle, and a lovely lavender fragrance wafted into the air. She breathed in deeply. "Oh, that's nice." She put a few drops in her hands, rubbed them together, and took another deep breath. Anne sighed with contentment.

"Feel better? Hope said this would help with any jitters."

"Yes. I do feel better." She took a deep breath of the calming scent.

I'm a grown woman. How bad can this be?

Chapter Nine

The short drive only heightened Anne's senses. Though she tried desperately to calm her nerves, they refused to listen and ignored her inner pleadings. If Kandi hadn't been driving, she would have turned around and gone home.

Kandi pulled into the parking lot. As usual, the local gathering spot looked to have a full crowd inside. Anne sat in the truck and glanced toward the door. Had it always looked that imposing?

This is it. I can do this. She bolstered her confidence and opened the door.

After exiting the truck, Anne faced Kandi. The young woman had the goofiest grin on her face.

"Thanks for bringing me, Kandi, and for all of your help today. I'm really thankful for all you've done." Anne stumbled as she took a step away from the truck. Kandi's three-inch heels were far from her usual choice of comfortable flats.

"You're welcome. You look terrific. Now go knock 'em dead." Kandi waved her off.

Anne gathered her courage and stepped tentatively

toward the entrance of the town's primary meeting hall. The large nondescript building held a restaurant, a community center, and in the back, a four-lane bowling alley. The building also held a craft beer pub and a small dance hall/theater space. She took a deep breath and pulled the heavy wooden door open.

The pub's interior was dark so Anne allowed her eyes to adjust for a moment. As she did, she noticed movement to her right.

A gentleman of at least ninety stood up. Actually, he pulled himself up and held on to the table. His scraggly gray beard covered much of what was an attempted smile, which was probably for the best since most of his teeth were missing.

He wore a red tie.

Seriously? How old does Kandi think I am? She smiled back at the man.

Her shoulders began to relax. *Actually, this may not be so bad after all. With all the medals he's wearing on his jacket, I bet I can learn a bunch of history. This might turn out to be a nice evening after all.*

As she took a step toward the older gentleman, another man stood. He was more her age, balding on top. He opened his jacket. He had on a red tie.

What the—?

To her left, two women stood. They opened their blazers to reveal red ties. Little by little, more people across the pub stood. All wore red ties.

Anne felt a light push on her back, propelling her into the midst of the room. She turned to see Kandi, now also sporting a red tie.

"Is this a practical joke?" Anne questioned Kandi.

"Not a joke." Kandi squeezed her arm. "You'll see."

She turned Anne to face the stage. The band—also wearing red ties— produced a resounding '*dut-dutta-da*' from their instruments. Balloons fell onto the stage. A banner hanging from the ceiling unfurled. It read "Welcome to Carolan Springs."

A silver-haired man made his way toward her. He took Anne's hands in a hearty shake. "We want to officially welcome you to Carolan Springs. This"—he gestured around the room—"is our town's welcome committee."

The tension Anne had been holding back released, and she broke out in hearty laughter. She smiled at everyone. "Thank you. This is the most memorable welcome I've ever received."

The pub responded with cheers, clapping, and a hoisting of mugs, glasses, and coffee cups.

"Oh, but the ceremony is not over." Kandi led her to the stage.

The mayor followed. "First, you must commit to this union." He moved next to her.

"Um, okay." Anne glanced out at the group, now clustered around the stage.

"Repeat after me."

The mayor recited a pledge, pausing occasionally to give Anne time to repeat his words. "I, Anne Freemont... do solemnly swear to uphold all the silly rules of my new town...and to carefully understand the importance of my role as citizen ambassador of my fair city...forever and ever, Scooby dooby doo."

Anne tried to repeat it with a straight face but

struggled to compose herself as she watched the audience try to stifle chuckles.

"The chalice!" yelled the mayor.

Someone bounded onto the stage and handed her a strange looking cup. The goblet was crafted from aspen wood and had the initials C and S carved into the side. Anne peered into it. Nothing strange. It looked like water. She took a sip. Carbonated spring water.

She chugged the rest of it down with gusto. After she finished, she held the cup upside down while everyone cheered. The mayor spoke. "And for the final piece of the initiation, Kandi, if you will do the honors."

Kandi pulled another red tie from her pocket and placed it over Anne's eyes. Then Anne was led outside. "Lean on me. I need you to sit. It's a scooter." Kandi's voice was calming.

Anne sat gingerly down onto a seat. Her arms were placed around someone.

"Hold on tight." A male voice she recognized. She grabbed onto the jacket. *Wait, was that? Yes, the smell of popcorn.* Warm hands enveloped hers as he made sure she had them securely wrapped around his waist. "Okay, here we go."

The scooter started up. Their pace was fairly slow and Anne relaxed. The distance to their destination was short. She felt them stop. Gentle hands helped her to her feet.

"Watch your–oh wait, you can't watch—just step lightly. You'll feel a board. It's four steps and then a landing." Sam held on to her arm and helped her to navigate.

A set of wooden steps echoed under Anne's feet.

She found herself standing on a sturdy surface. Hands removed the tie from her eyes. As she blinked, she looked up to see the town's welcome sign now lit up against the night sky. The number showing the population of thirty-seven hundred now lacked the last zero. A young man appeared and handed her a paintbrush with instruction to paint a straight line on the end.

Thirty-seven hundred and one. She made the stroke on the board. Anne fought back the big lump in her throat and the tears that sprung to her eyes. But for once, these were tears of joy. She had not just moved to another town, she had come home to a welcoming family. Never in her life had she felt so much care and affection being showered upon her.

"Anne Freemont," the mayor bellowed, "you are now an official citizen of Carolan Springs."

Everyone cheered. She smiled back at the crowd. Anne felt a squeeze on her hand. She turned to see Kandi.

"Forgive me?" Kandi cocked her head in query.

She pulled the young woman into a warm embrace. "Of course! Kandi, that was probably the best surprise ever. And honestly, much better than a blind date. And you were right, I do thank you."

"Listen, I'd love to stay, but I've got to go to a meeting about an upcoming homesteading fair. You could come with me." Kandi waved toward a group, who motioned at her to hurry.

"Run along. I'll be fine." Anne waved Kandi off.

She looked back at the sign. When Anne had first considered moving to a new place, she'd known she wanted somewhere small. Someplace where, hopefully, many people wouldn't know her. Finding Carolan Springs had felt like a sign. In this case, a real sign. She'd packed up her east coast life and headed west to the Rockies. She had found her home. Anne ran her hands up and down her arms.

"Here. You must be chilled." A warm jacket full of masculine scent came across her shoulders.

"Thank you, Sam. It is a bit chilly."

"You look really lovely tonight—if no one told you."

"Thank you." *Is he flirting with me? Nah. He's at least seven, maybe, ten years younger.*

"Hate to see you go home after thinking you were going out for dinner. Hungry?"

Anne's stomach rumbled.

"I'll take that as a yes. Listen, we can stay here, or I know a great place. It's a bit out of the way but the chef is pretty good, if I do say so myself."

She faced him. "Why not."

"Great. Let's take this scooter back to Sally. They thought it would be more fun than a car. Then we can head out." They reached the pub just as the sheriff's vehicle pulled up next to them.

"Sheriff. How's it going? You missed the welcome party."

The officer exited the vehicle. He grunted.

Sam waited while Anne dismounted, almost falling when her heel caught in the gravel. She grabbed onto the back to steady herself.

"You been drinking, Ms. Freemont?" The sheriff gave Anne a once-over.

"No. My heel got stuck."

His responding look said he'd heard every excuse in the book.

"How's the Roger's case coming?" Sam removed the keys from the scooter.

"I don't talk about cases in front of witnesses or possible suspects."

Anne raised herself to her full high-heeled height, but she was still a good half head lower than the sheriff.

"Are you saying I'm a witness or that you consider me a suspect? Because if it's the latter, I had absolutely no reason whatsoever to kill that man."

"Aren't you very friendly with Kandi Jenkins?"

"Well, yes. But what has that got to do with anything?" She placed her hands on her hips and tried to remain steady while standing on tippy-toes. The shoes were really starting to pinch and hurt. "You need to quit going after Kandi and get serious about finding the real killer."

He bristled, but didn't reply.

She stared up at him.

He stared down at her.

He broke the unspoken stand-off. "How'd you get the bruise on your head, Ms. Freemont?"

She reached up and touched her temple. "I got it..." Dang. She stopped quickly.

"I believe you got the one on your head when you were trespassing on a crime scene after the murder. Isn't that correct?" He rested his hand on his gun holster.

"And that was after you had a nasty fall in his backyard a few days before the victim was murdered." He took a step toward her.

"You think I killed a man because of a fall I took into his compost pile?" She wanted to retreat but feared falling.

"People are strange, Ms. Freemont. You'd be surprised at the reasons people give to justify killing someone. Just last summer, old lady Pepper killed her husband, supposedly over toilet paper. Seems they'd fought for fifty years over which way it should go on the roller. She said she'd had enough. The next time he said, 'Over,' she hit him over the head with an iron frying pan. So you see, murder can happen to the best of us."

He was kidding, right? "Oh, you're just pulling—"

"Just what? I'd be careful if I were you, Ms. Freemont. You best remember you're speaking to an officer of the law."

"Come on, Carson." With a hard stare from the sheriff, Sam stopped. "I mean, Sheriff Carson. I'm sure Ms. Freemont wants the killer caught like the rest of us do."

"That's right. In fact, I have my own suspect list." *Shoot. Why did I say that out loud?*

"You do, do you? Are you a private detective, Ms. Freemont?" He stepped closer.

"No. But…" She inched back, stopping when her heel twisted.

"That is the correct answer. No, you are not. You don't know what you are doing, and you need to stick to doing"—he appraised her—"whatever it is that you do. Leave the detective work to the professionals."

Was he judging her by the heels she wore? She should never have let Kandi convince her the dress needed heels instead of ballet flats. She bristled at his appraisal. Well, she'd show him what she could do.

"Fine! I'll just figure out the suspect list on my own."

"Ms. Freemont, do you know that you can be arrested for interfering in a murder investigation?"

"I'm not interfering."

"Good. Let's keep it that way." He tipped his hat, "Ms. Freemont, Sam." He strode toward the pub.

Anne sighed in frustration. *That man is incorrigible.*

Chapter Ten

Sam chuckled. "Let's go and get rid of that *hangry* Anne."

"What?"

"You know when you get hungry and then you get angry? Come on. The night's a-wasting." He opened the truck door for her.

Anne slid onto the brown seat. Like the man driving the truck, it had a scent all its own. Besides popcorn, another smell permeated the interior. She couldn't place it. Animal, maybe. Anne leaned against the seat. The day's hectic pace had finally caught up with her. A wave of fatigue hit as she stifled a yawn. Covering her mouth with her hand, she glanced out the passenger window. They passed the county line.

"Um, is this place not in town?" She appraised Sam as he focused on the road.

"Oh, it's at my house. Hope that's okay." Before she had a chance to respond, Sam hit his high beams and down-shifted his truck. The lights shone on a small white mailbox, the only indication of a passage between the trees. They began the rough jaunt down the potholed lane. "Sorry for the bumps. I'm planning on regrading the road, but I can't get to it until next weekend."

Great. He's taking me to his place. What if he's Ralph's killer? Or a rapist? She surreptitiously glanced at her door. The handle still looked intact, so that was good. She inched closer to it. What did she have in her purse she could use as defense? Lipstick and some breath mints didn't seem to rank high on the protection list. She did have her phone. Luckily, she still held her purse. She silently opened it and searched inside.

Just then *his* phone beeped. "Oops. Sorry. Just a second." He answered through his vehicle speakers. "Dispatch."

A muted woman's voice.

Sam responded. "Oh, hi, Miss Faith. How are you doing?" He listened.

Anne could hear what sounded like a jumble of words. "Ralph…sleeping. I like snow."

"Are you at home? Is Hope there? Hello? Hello?" Only silence.

Sam's face tensed, and then relaxed when Hope came on the line.

After Hope spoke, Sam replied, "No need to apologize. Have a good night, Hope." He ended the call. "Sorry about that. I'm on dispatch for the night. Okay, now what was I saying?"

This couldn't be any worse. My possible killer is the one manning 9-1-1 calls. Reality calmed her suspicion. *Geez. What's wrong with you! He's no more a killer than you're a great opera singer. This thing with Ralph has you looking at everyone as a murderer in the making.* She thought back to Hope's words. Had her fragile mind mixed up his death and sleeping?

"You were talking about the…" Anne motioned to the road.

Sam interrupted. "Here we are."

The truck emerged from the dark stand of trees into a broad clearing. A small cabin appeared, lights glowing in the windows and on the porch. Stretching beyond the bungalow, a huge lake glimmered with moonlight. It looked like something out of a painting.

Anne leaned forward and took in the view. "Wow. This is beautiful."

"Yes. I love it here." He pulled the keys from the ignition and turned to face her. "Heads up. Before you get out of the truck, be careful of Hank."

"Hank?"

Just then a golden retriever bounded off the porch. Sam opened his door. They tussled with one another before he commanded the dog to sit and stay. "Okay, you can get out now."

Anne exited her side and went around to where the dog sat. "Is it okay if I pet him?"

"Sure. He loves people, but I don't want him jumping on you." She clumsily bent down and ruffled the dog's ears. He responded with a wet tongue down her arm.

"Hank, in," Sam commanded.

Without hesitation, the dog ran to the porch and disappeared off to the side. Sam offered Anne his arm. "Wouldn't want you falling in those things." He glanced at her shoes.

"They're Kandi's, and truth be told, I'm ready for them to be off my feet."

He escorted her around the back. "I rarely use the front door." He kicked a chewed tennis ball from their path. The rear of the cabin had a deck built up over the water. The back door stood open, and the golden retriever now sprawled onto a rolled rag rug, a dog toy in his mouth.

"Did you leave the door open?" Anne gawked.

"Don't look so surprised. I knew I'd be gone for a bit. Wanted Hank to be able to get outside if nature called. We're a small town. Not many people lock their doors. We have little to no crime, so many just see it as a senseless hassle." He stood back to allow her to enter. "Plus, an open door isn't that much different than a closed one. If someone really wants to get in, they'll find a way."

Anne shivered, knowing what he said was true. Still, having locked doors gave her peace of mind.

"Don't worry. Hank wouldn't be so friendly without me here." He nodded toward the dog. "Right, boy?" The dog dropped the toy and wagged his tail.

Anne entered to find a bright kitchen, dining room, and living room combination. Two doors opened off to the side. At the far end of the room, a set of stairs headed up to a second floor. Another set of stairs mirroring the upper ones looked like they led down to a basement level.

"This is nice. Very cozy."

"It's good for me and him. Huh, boy?" The golden

raised his head and wagged his tail at Sam. "Got any pets?"

"No. No pets." Anne shrugged out of the jacket Sam had let her borrow.

"Well, you should remedy that." He set down a bowl of dog food Hank ignored.

Anne looked around. "Do you want help with anything?"

"Naw. That's okay. Wouldn't want you to get something on that dress. You just sit back and let me wait on you." He pulled out a jug from the refrigerator and held it up. "I've been hooked on hot cider lately. Want some?"

"Sounds good. Thank you." She perched on the edge of a chair and slid the high heels off her feet. Wiggling her toes, she realized, if nothing else, she could use the shoes Kandi let her borrow to protect herself. No wonder they called them killer shoes with those spikes on the end. *You've got to rein in your wild imagination before it gets you in trouble. And no more true crime documentaries or detective shows.*

Sliding into the chair, she pulled her legs up under her. Sam poured the golden liquid into a pot on the stove to simmer. The smell of apple and cinnamon filled the air. She sighed with contentment. "I'm going to go get out of my work clothes. I'll be back in a jiff." He pointed to one of the doors. "There's a bathroom if you want to wash your hands." Sam sprinted over to the stairs and took them two at a time. His trim frame coupled with his energy and strength showed he clearly kept himself in top physical shape.

Anne took advantage of the time. In the bathroom, she washed her hands and then applied some more lip gloss. While she waited for him to return, she rested her head on the back of the chair. *Sam's a nice guy and certainly no killer.* She closed her eyes. The town's welcome had been so thoughtful. A home-cooked meal would be a great way to end the evening.

"Tired?" He'd returned without her hearing. He moved to the kitchen and poured the warm cider into a cup. She joined him at the island dividing the rooms and perched on a barstool.

He handed the cider to her. "Here's to new friendships." He held up his mug. She responded in kind. "I better get you fed, so I can get you home. You'll need your sleep. I've got a feeling Kandi will be contacting you tomorrow about helping out at her fair."

"Her fair?" Anne took a sip. "Wow. This is really good cider."

"Thanks. I made it." He poured some into a dark blue mug he pulled from an open shelf.

"You made it?"

"Yep. With my line of work, you spend a whole lot of time sitting around. We've got so many apples around these parts that I decided to make it from scratch. I call it 'Veronica's Cider' in honor of my mom."

"That's so sweet. I bet your mom loves it." She took another sip.

"I think she would have." He opened the refrigerator and pulled out a closed container. "She died before she got to test it."

"Oh, I'm so very sorry."

"It's sad. But it brought me home. I never thought I'd return. But, I belong here." He pulled food from the refrigerator.

"Really, please let me help." Anne moved off the stool.

"Okay, hold on." He went upstairs and returned with a pair of wool socks and one of his flannel shirts. "Sorry, I don't have an apron. But this should protect your dress and keep your feet and legs warm"

As Anne put on the clothing, Sam filled the sink with water and stuck the corn in it, shuck and all. Anne returned and raised her mug. "Here's to finding Ralph's killer."

"Not great dinner conversation." He handed her some washed spinach, red onion, and feta for making the salad. "Here's a bowl. The knives are in that drawer and the cutting board is over there." As Anne gathered her tools, Sam drew out a filleted trout from a refrigerated container.

"I'm just worried about Kandi. I can't see her hurting anyone, much less killing someone." She put the spinach in the bowl and started slicing the onion.

"Oops. Better get this going. Got sidetracked." With a quick flip, the entire glass wall fell back on itself in accordion fashion and the deck became an extension of the living space.

"Oh, that's wonderful." Anne clapped her hands.

"Cost me a hunk of money, but it was on my top ten list when I built here. I enjoy the cooler temps but if it gets too cold, let me know and we'll go back inside. Usually the fireplace does a great job of keeping things toasty."

Outdoors, he started up the fireplace and added a couple logs. Next to it, he turned on the gas grill. Before long, Anne's mouth watered as cooking odors wafted on the air. As they waited on the food, Sam rolled the dining table outdoors in front of the fireplace. Working in unison, they placed the cooked food on the table. He handed her a dish of melted butter, lemon, and dill. Anne drizzled some on her fish, which practically melted in her mouth. "Ummmmm. This is delicious."

"Caught it today. From out there." He motioned toward the lake.

He paused. "Listen, I'm not trying to dissuade you about Kandi. But no one knows how they will react when certain situations come up. Whoever killed Ralph meant it. That axe went straight to his vital organs. Kandi is the right height which lines up with the wound. Her prints are on the axe. The DNA is there. All the evidence points to her."

"Okay, I'll give you that. But would you hide the axe in your own yard if you were the killer?"

"Well. Let's think about that." He wiped butter from his chin with a checkered cloth napkin. "There's two ways to look at the situation. One, I'm the killer and I goofed big time in trying to get rid of the murder weapon. Two, I put the weapon there in order to make the police think it was planted, hoping to take suspicion off me."

"I guess that makes sense. But someone else could have planted the weapon there. Right?" Anne used her knife to scoop some corn onto her fork.

"Of course. The problem is that there were only two sets of fingerprints on the weapon. Ralph's and Kandi's."

"But that's because Kandi grabbed the axe when Ralph said he'd kill her chicken."

Sam arched his eyebrows. "Ralph threatened to kill her chicken? Maybe she killed Ralph?"

"But he didn't. He just told her to keep the chickens out of his garden. She'd have to have a better motive than that."

"I'd rather not speculate. Or talk about it without any facts." He buttered some bread and took a bite.

"Look, I'm just saying, I think there are others with more of a motive to kill Ralph."

He held up his hand as he swallowed. "Like who? You don't know all that many people here in town yet. Plus, as I've already said, all the evidence points to Kandi. Also, this isn't the first time these two have clashed." He motioned to the basket. "More bread?"

Anne shook her head. "While that may be true, there are others who stand to gain. What about Stewart?"

"Ralph's nephew?" Sam shook his head. "I've known Stewart forever. He's a good guy."

"Okay. But I saw Stewart storm off from Ralph's not too long before he was killed. Maybe his uncle wouldn't help with more money for his business. He stands to inherit part of Ralph's property which is double the size of my lot or Kandi's."

"Hmmm. Interesting. But that's still another motive for Kandi." The golden joined the pair, looking up at Sam. "Down, Hank." The dog circled before flopping down next to the chair.

"What do you mean?" Anne set her fork down.

"For a long time, Kandi has wanted to create an

agritourism industry here. If she had Ralph's place, it'd be another step toward making it come true. In a town this size, it's not often property comes up for sale. Yours was one of the exceptions."

"Going with your premise, then why didn't she just buy my house?"

"You know yourself it needs a lot of work."

"Tell me about it. The entire upper story probably has to be gutted. As of right now, I'm living in the kitchen and maid's quarters. But I also got the place for a song. So Kandi could have bought it and fixed it up just like I'm doing. It should triple in value once repairs and updates are complete."

"True. However, why not buy a place that's ready to go? Plus, no dealing with your husband harping about the bad deal you made."

"Sounds like you're not a Jeff fan either," Anne replied.

"Jeff grew up alongside all of us, but he couldn't wait to leave and hit the big city. He works with some kind of financial organization but ended up getting fired. Not long after he got back he started seeing Kandi. Her grandfather made no bones about his dislike for Jeff. Then once Kandi's mom showed up, and the whole inheritance thing, he never left. Everyone knows he married Kandi for a chance to get his hands on her mother's money, but you can't tell her that. She defends Jeff no matter what. He's all about the money. The more, the better." He sighed.

"You don't suppose Jeff killed Ralph, and Kandi's covering for him?"

He sat back in his chair. "That's an intriguing thought.

But I can't see Kandi doing anything like that." He leaned in. "There's been some rumors he has a girlfriend up in Denver. I really feel sorry for Kandi. She is the true epitome of the saying that love is blind.

"Hold on." Sam returned with two ramekins. "Egg custard."

"Yum." Anne slid the spoon into the rich dessert. "Oh, wow. You really are a wonderful cook. You'll make some lady a great husband one day."

"We'll see."

A thought occurred to Anne. "What about Hope?"

"What about her?"

"Well, you're both interested in medicine, and you're about the same age, I would think. How old are you anyway?"

"Does that matter?" His voice came across rough.

The question took her aback. "No. I was just saying you're close to the same age, that's all." She took a bite of the custard.

"Don't get me wrong. Hope's a great lady. But she's not the one for me."

"Okay. Sorry I brought it up."

He stared off toward the lake. Something hit Anne on the nose. Soft and light. Another hit. Then another. She looked up. "It's snowing!" she yelled gleefully. Snowflakes tickled her face. Hank ran to her side, dancing.

"Looks like we're getting our first snowfall early this year."

"Does that happen often?" She tipped her head to the sky.

"It's Colorado. When it comes to the weather,

anything can happen. That's what I love about it." He moved his chair back. "Let's get this stuff inside, and then I'll take you home."

They cleared away the detritus of their meal. "That was delicious. I can't remember the last time I had such a wonderful meal. And such a delightful dinner companion too."

"Thanks for the compliments. I don't think we were expecting any major accumulation so this will probably quit soon but just in case probably best to get you home."

Anne reluctantly put the high heels back on her feet. In the meantime, Sam shut off the fireplace, moved the table inside, and closed the window wall.

"Here." He held out the jacket she'd worn earlier. He grabbed another from a closet.

"Bye, Hank. Keep the home fires burning." The retriever raised his head and grinned.

"Did he just smile?" Anne patted the dog's head.

"Goldens always look like that." Sam patted the dog's head. "Isn't that right, bud?"

They crossed over the deck toward the front porch. Already the ground out to the truck looked wet. "Hold on." Sam moved toward a shed. He returned lugging a large cut sheet of plywood. He laid it out next to the bottom step. Motioning at her to wait, he maneuvered the truck so the plywood covered the wet ground. He came around the truck and opened the passenger door. "At your service." He bowed.

Anne stepped onto the wood and entered the truck. "Thanks."

"Don't want you mad at me for ruining your—

Kandi's—shoes." He moved to the driver's side, and they began the bumpy ride to the main road.

Anne took one last backward glance at the cabin. "You really have a nice place here."

"You should see it when the sun sets over the water." He turned and smiled at her.

She smiled back. *What's a little harmless flirting? The man is handsome, a great cook, a good conversationalist, and very charming. He's the one who can help me find Ralph's killer.*

They had reached the main intersection. He looked both ways and pulled out.

"I'll have to come back to see that sunset some day." Up ahead, something caught her attention. She pointed at something on her side of the road. "Look! What's that?"

Sam down-shifted. He turned on the high beams and leaned forward, straining to see through the darkness and falling snow. In an instant, he pulled off to the shoulder and shoved the gear into park. "Wait here!" He shot out of the door and sprinted in front of the truck.

Anne tentatively opened her door. Then looking at the wet, snowy ground, she decided to stay put. She craned her body out as far as she could.

A car had run off the road and now rested half in and half out of a shallow bar ditch. The car's red taillights were what she'd seen. Steam rose from the engine, twirling in a strange dance with the snowflakes that now fell heavily from the sky. She squinted. It looked like a person slumped over the steering wheel.

"No!" It had finally registered what she was seeing. Anne knew whose car it was.

Eliza's.

Chapter Eleven

After the ambulance had left with Eliza, Sam took Anne home.

Had Eliza missed the turn? Had someone run her off the road? If they had, did it have to do with Ralph's murder? Did Eliza know something that someone didn't want her to remember?

The adrenaline rush subsided and exhaustion found her. Her eyelids drooped. Better to go to sleep and think about everything tomorrow. Nothing could be done tonight. Yet, Anne slept fitfully.

Her dreams were a mash-up of so many things.

Kandi grabbing the axe from Ralph.

A shady figure running across Ralph's property.

Eliza's car covered in designer gloves.

Falling into the compost pile.

Being walked on by a chicken.

Something scratchy licking her face.

This isn't part of the dream. Something is really licking my face.

Her raised hand met with something furry. Anne shot up in bed as a black ball of fur tumbled to her lap. A tiny kitten gazed up at her and mewed softly. The kitten circled around a couple of times before curling into a tight ball. Purring commenced.

A giggle. Kandi stood at the door.

Don't these people ever knock around here?

"Surprise!" Kandi chirped in an annoying morning-person voice.

Groaning, Anne fell back on the bed and pulled the quilt over her head.

Maybe, just maybe, she'll go away. She felt body weight settle next to her.

"Yum. This coffee is so, so good. Guess I'll just have to, *like*, drink it myself."

Anne mumbled through the covers, "Over my dead body."

"That can be arranged. You know, *like*, I'm a scary axe murderer who kills people for fun."

Anne sat up, pushed the covers down, and accepted the steaming mug. Kandi had made it just the way she liked it with a hint of cream and a touch of sweetness. Gone were the days of having to endure black coffee so as not to put on an ounce of weight. She fluffed her pillows and sat back against the headboard. "So to what do I owe this early morning honor?" She took another satisfying swallow. "And what's with the kitten?"

"Sam told me what happened last night with Eliza. He didn't have your cell phone number. He wanted me to check up on you."

"That's nice, but I'm fine. Just a bit of a shock. First Ralph and now Eliza's accident. I came here to get away from the big city and bad things." She looked down at the purring kitten. "Still, what about this little thing?"

"My tabby had a run-in with a friendly tom a while back. He got in, or she got out." Kandi stuck her hair behind an ear. "Anyway, now I've got these kittens needing a good home, and you need a mouser."

"A mouser?" Anne frowned, distracted by the almost empty cup.

Without a word, Kandi took the cup and set off for the kitchen. Anne picked up the sleeping kitten and held it next to her ear. The purring increased as she stroked the black fur.

Kandi returned. Anne set the kitten down and took the cup. "You really are sweet. Strange but sweet." She smiled at the girl.

"Ha. Ha. Where was I? Oh yeah, *like*…" She caught herself. "Winter is coming soon."

"Winter. That explains it." Anne savored the warmth of the cup she held.

"Good. Glad you know, then." Kandi sat down at the end of the bed.

"Um, no. I have no idea what you are talking about. I was being facetious."

"You were, *like*, being…wait…that sounds familiar."

"Never mind. Why do I need a mouser? Ohhh…" She glanced around the room.

"Finally! The light bulb comes on at last." Kandi plopped down on the bed.

"Look, I just woke up but I don't want a cat. If I see a mouse, I'll simply put out a trap."

"Listen, you're not living upstairs. There are lots of

holes, and even though it's not being heated much, it's warmer than outside. They come in, make their nests and, *like*, soon you've got a huge mouse village. Before you know it, they're singing YMCA."

Anne struggled to not spit her coffee all over her bed as images of Village Mice in various costume danced through her head.

"A cat will make sure that doesn't happen. Those mice know there is no room at this inn." Kandi smiled. "Plus, you, *like*, need a companion. You're all alone in this big old house."

"Thanks for reminding me." Anne certainly liked the solitude and running her own life, but with a murderer on the loose, it had made the old house a tad less inviting.

"You're welcome." Kandi smoothed down the bedcover with her hand.

This girl is really naïve. Anne watched the young woman. *No, she just thinks the best of everyone and everything. Kandi is fresh air to my stale, cynical spirit.*

"Oh, wait. You're being, *like*, what was it again? Facetious!" Kandi laughed. "I'm already learning so much from you." She hopped off the bed. "Well, got to go."

"Wait!" Anne yelled in vain as the back door slammed. "I don't want any kitten!"

The tiny creature looked up at her and meowed pitifully. She raised the kitten so they were eye to eye. "Okay, fine. But this is just a trial. You hear me? You don't catch any mice and you're out of here." Anne placed the black ball of fluff in her lap. She'd almost fallen back to sleep when the back door banged open again and Kandi reappeared. "Oh, I forgot. Meeting at my house at ten to discuss the homesteading fair and who's going to do what. See you there."

"Can't make it." Anne yawned.

"What do you mean you can't make it? I need everyone to help." Kandi planted her fists on her hips. "You can't help? Oh, okay. Sorry. Didn't realize, *like*, your schedule was so full." She stood there, waiting.

"Fine. Fine. I'll be there. I'm just not sure how much I can help. I'm trying to get things ready for the winter. Next week, I'm interviewing carpenters and repairmen."

"Great. See you then. I left a bit of kibble and a package of chicken livers in the fridge for the kitten." The young woman moved to the door.

"Kandi, hold on!" Anne placed the kitten on the bed and swung her legs over the side. "How did you get in my house?"

"Oh, simple. I just, *like*, used the key on top of the door frame. Everyone does that here in case someone forgets and locks their door. Did you forget?" Kandi cocked her head.

"No. I didn't forget. I lock my doors. You know there *is* a murderer on the loose!"

Kandi frowned. "Oh gosh. I forgot about that." Her forehead crinkled. Then a smile played across her lips. "But since I'm supposed to be the murderer, I guess I'm, *like*, okay. They wouldn't want to murder me because then people would know they're, *like*, the murderer. So I'm safe!" She brushed her hair from her face and pulled an elastic band off her wrist. With a quick, familiar action, she pulled her hair into a high ponytail. "See you at ten!"

As Kandi bounded out of the room, Anne shook her head. "Yep, one brick short."

By the time Anne arrived at Kandi's, a line of cars had formed in front of the house. Inside, a cluster of men and women were either piling food on plates or pouring coffee into various mugs set on the counter. Jeff made his way halfway down the back kitchen staircase, shook his head, turned, and hurried back upstairs.

Chairs were set up in a semicircle. People sat with plates perched precariously on their laps. A whiteboard stood next to the fireplace. The group of people hushed as Kandi entered and strode across the room. Grabbing Anne's hand, she led her in front of the group.

"Everyone, this is Anne. She bought the old place across the cul-de-sac." She motioned in the direction of Anne's house. She was, *like*, with me when I found Ralph." Kandi shivered and Anne instinctively placed a hand on her arm. Kandi beamed up at Anne.

A couple whispered to each other.

"Are we going to get started?" an elderly man with salt-and-pepper hair growled at the group. "I got work to do."

Next to him, a petite woman patted his hand. "Now,

Stanley, you know we set aside time for this. Those boys out working will do just fine."

He harrumphed and grabbed his Carhartt jacket as it slid toward the floor.

Kandi smiled at the group. "Thank you all for coming. As many of you know I'm, *like*, so excited to be this year's chair of our annual homesteading fair. I—"

An older woman with hair dyed bright orange interrupted Kandi. "I think we need to cancel this event."

What's up with older women and the stock Halloween hair colors? Oh patron saint of old ladies, please don't let me pick orange, black, or even blue hair color when I get older.

The orange-haired lady continued. "I'm just going to say it again. I don't know why we need any homesteading fair. We got the county fair every year over in Larimer County."

"Ms. Alice, you know that is an hour and a half away from Carolan Springs." Kandi turned to the woman. "This is to create an avenue to showcase our growing agritourism efforts. It brings tourists."

"I don't want no dad-burn tourists coming here," Stanley interjected. "We got enough of them city folk moving here already." He stared pointedly at Anne.

Kandi sighed. "Now, Mr. Culpepper, you need to sell all those great apples from your orchard."

Anne could almost see the wheels turning in Mr. Culpepper's mind about possible profits to be gained.

"And Ms. Alice, like, everyone knows you make the most beautiful winning quilts in the county."

Alice beamed and sat up straighter.

One of the younger individuals in the group spoke

up. She was half of a couple that looked to be about Kandi's age. "I really think this is a great opportunity for us. We could use some help—"

"In my day, we didn't gripe about help, we just did it," the older man interrupted.

His wife patted his hand again, "Stanley."

The young woman continued, "Our goats take a lot of work and, besides milking, there's making cheese and soap. Being able to sell product and also do some teaching will really be helpful when…"

Hope appeared in the doorway. She held on to her mother's hand. As Faith scoped the room with her gaze, it landed on the young woman who'd been talking. She let go of Hope's hand and walked directly to the young woman.

"Twins." She put her hands on the woman's stomach. "One of each." She smiled up at the woman, kissed her on the forehead, and turned back to Hope.

Everyone turned to the young couple, and then a middle-aged woman jumped up. "Is this true, Karen?"

The young woman smiled shyly and then broke out in a big grin, as she took her husband's hand. "We're pregnant."

The group broke out in applause. Congratulations were given and received.

When everyone had settled back down, Kandi brought the group to order.

After much staring in Anne's direction, a woman had excused herself and gone out toward the kitchen.

"Listen, we need to discuss who is going to do what,

what types of events and presentations we're going to have, and—"

A woman's squeal stopped Kandi from continuing.

"I knew it. I knew it was you!" The woman's excitement gathered steam as she addressed Anne.

"What do you mean, Velma?" Kandi looked back and forth from the woman to Anne.

Oh no. Anne focused intently on her lap.

"It's her! Caroline Tenet!" She pointed to her iPad screen. "I just had to check for sure. Oh, I'm so excited. A celebrity in our town!"

"Her name is Anne Freemont," Kandi retorted.

Velma ignored her. "If I go get my book, will you sign it?" She didn't wait for an answer but burst out the front door. The sound of a car starting up could be heard.

Everyone stared at Anne.

Suddenly Kandi's eyes came into focus as her mind made the connection. She stared at Anne. "You're the author of all those homesteading books?" Her hands shook.

"Who is she?" Stanley leaned toward his wife.

"A book writer."

"Oh, is that all? Jimmy crack corn," he sniffled.

"Not *just* a book writer." The anger could be heard in Kandi's voice. "She's like the queen of homesteading. She has a huge farm in Virginia." Her voice was shaking. Vitriol poured from her. "What? Are you doing, *like*, research for another book? Is that why you've changed your appearance?"

"No. No, you have it all wrong." Anne moved toward Kandi. The group looked on in ponderous anticipation.

Kandi ran from the room and up the stairs.

"Excuse me." Anne followed Kandi. The buzz of the group's voices followed her.

Upstairs, Kandi ran into a room. Off to the other side, Jeff sat in his office. On seeing Anne, he mouthed, *Good riddance* and shut his door.

Jerk. I'd like to bean you over the head.

Anne knocked on the door. "Kandi, please, let me explain."

"Go. Away."

"Look, I'm sorry. It's not that I was hiding…okay, so yes, I wasn't telling anyone about who I was, but I was doing it for a reason. Please, let me…"

The door opened. Kandi appeared smaller somehow, and her face was blotched red from crying. "You must have been laughing the whole time. Every time I said something about my chickens, or the gardens, or anything, you must have had a good long laugh."

"I didn't. Yes, I already knew much of what you shared, but I wasn't trying to be mean. I just needed time."

"Time? Time!" Her voice squeaked, as it rose. "For what? To let me make more of a fool of myself? Me thinking I was helping you, and all the time you're an expert."

"You were—*are* helping me. Please, Kandi, forgive me. I'm sorry."

"You're all alike. I hate you!" She slammed the door shut.

Anne raised her hand to knock again, and then let it drop instead. "I'm sorry," she whispered.

Anne trudged down the stairs. While she'd hoped to avoid the group, they were now in the kitchen. Some were washing dishes, while others dried them. Another group stood out on the porch. Heads turned her direction. No one spoke. She pulled her tweed coat from the hook by the door and, without making any eye contact with anyone, headed out the door.

So much for a new start.

Chapter Twelve

In the first few days following the announcement, Anne had kept to her house. She discovered that she'd become the star of the town newspaper with a front page headline, CELEBRITY UNCOVERED IN CAROLAN SPRINGS.

She could only hope and pray the people driving by her house and pointing would soon stop. Why had she thought that a change in appearance and returning to her maiden name would provide enough privacy?

Yet, what hurt worse than the media attention was the rift between her and Kandi. How had this silly girl come to mean so much to her?

Trying her best to stay away from any cameras or the media, Anne had used the privacy afforded by Ralph's property to go to Kandi's when cabin fever struck. Sadly, Kandi wouldn't answer the door. The last time, she'd been met by Jeff at the back door who informed her with glee in his voice, "Kandi doesn't want to see you."

Anne couldn't hide forever. She would have to go back out into the world. Plus, she wanted to visit Eliza again. Gathering her hair up into a hat and putting on a pair of Ray-Bans, she headed for the detached garage. She opened the garage door. Inside the musty shed, she climbed into the old pickup she'd purchased before moving to the Springs. Taking in a deep breath of courage, she drove the truck down the drive.

A few people loitered by the curb edge, but another van with a large national logo now sat there also.

Oh, no. Not mainstream media.

She sighed deeply. Better to get it over with now.

She shifted the truck into park and got out. Walking briskly toward the assembled group of local media, onlookers, and the larger van, she kept her head up and shoulders back. The professionals quickly eclipsed Sally, the town paper's junior reporter, with their barrage of questions.

"Ladies and gentlemen," Anne said. "I've only got a short amount of time to respond to a few questions. Sally, what can I answer for you?"

A microphone was thrust into Sally's face by the reporter from the larger conglomerate.

"Um, um," Sally stuttered, obviously realizing she'd just become part of the story. "Ms. Freemont, why did you choose Carolan Springs?"

"Great question, Sally." Anne smiled at the young woman.

Sally turned and beamed at the photojournalist's camera.

"I wanted to find a place full of great people, and I did that in discovering Carolan Springs. It's one of the best towns in this country. I would like—"

The national reporter cut her off. "Ms. Freemont, is it true that your divorce caused you to have a breakdown?"

Another reporter picked up the thread. "Did you move here because you couldn't handle city life?"

Anger rose as acid in her throat. *Don't let them goad you, Anne.*

She smiled. The fake sentiment came surprisingly easy, with as much practice as she'd had with her ex-husband.

"As to your question, I think what you *meant* to say is that I had a break-*out*. People who have read my books will understand my desire to get back to a simpler life."

The reporter from KBC jostled for a better position. "So there's no truth to the rumor you're upset over Senate candidate Duke Tenet and his wife's announcement?"

"Announcement?" *Shoot. You goofed. Now you've opened the door.*

"Yes, her pregnancy." The woman leered. "They're expecting a baby."

"Well I, I ..." she stuttered, "I obviously didn't know, as I do not keep up with their lives." Anne struggled to make her voice light. "But a hearty congratulations to them." She gritted her teeth and smiled.

Sally had finally found her voice again and thankfully changed the subject. "Ms. Freemont, are you planning on writing any more books?" She preened for the cameras, flipping her blond hair over her shoulder.

Memories fought to the surface as Anne pushed them down. She struggled to talk as she took in what the journalist had said. *Breathe. Breathe.* Her chest felt heavy and she could feel her cheeks flushing. She took a deep breath. "I have my hands full now with the restoration of my house, but who knows—"

The woman from KBC cut in, not satisfied with the less sensational tone the conversation had taken. "I heard you were on the scene of a murder and actually know the murderer."

"I don't know any murderer. The woman accused of the crime is a wonderful young lady who was in the wrong place at the wrong time. I'm sure she will be fully vindicated. The town is mourning one of its longtime residents." She stared pointedly at the woman. "The town needs space to grieve."

The reporter took up the scent. "Did you move here to grieve the loss of your marriage and upper-class lifestyle?"

"No. I…" *Be careful, remember the NDA.* "I have no further comments. I must be going."

She turned and headed back to the truck. Cameras flashed around her as she exited the driveway. She fought her desire to run over the entire group. As she headed out on the road to town, her body shook. Anne checked her mirror to make sure no one had followed her. The memories and emotions she'd fought for so long now came in wave after wave. Her hands began shaking so she pulled over to the side of the road and shut off the truck.

Only then did she allow the deep sobs to come.

Chapter Twelve

Eighteen years ago.

Her first meeting with Robert Duke Harrison Tenet. A whirlwind engagement had led to an extravagant wedding.

Soon enough Duke charmed his way into a partnership with a prestigious law firm. However, Duke's long days spent working on litigation left Anne with lots of free time. On a whim, she'd attended a lecture on the growth of local food and the rise of urban homesteaders and backyard farming. She'd fallen in love with the idea of "country living in the city."

Before she knew it, they'd bought a second house in the country and she was writing about all things associated with backyard farming. As Duke spent more time away, Anne focused on writing. She chose a tongue-in-cheek pseudonym of Anne Tenet. Duke had no idea it was because she felt like Marie Antoinette on her little farm, pretending to live a different life. Later, her publisher had suggested Caroline Tenet—a combination of her first and middle names.

But as years crept by, Anne's internal clock ticked louder and louder. She desperately wanted to become a mother. Duke would convince her to wait 'just one more year.' It had been after another dinner that she had brought it up once again. "Duke, I'm in my late thirties. Time's slipping away."

"No need to rush." He focused on a text from his phone.

"Well, actually, there is. I'm pregnant." She laid her hands on her stomach.

Startled, he looked at her with a shocked gaze and said nothing. Finally, he stood and came over and kissed her. A ping on his phone stopped the moment. "I've got to go into the office." He left without looking back.

Dread gnawed at her and she shivered.

On Friday they'd held a small party. Anne was talking with her friend when Duke came over with a tray of drinks.

"Honey, do you think, I hate to ask—"

"Of course. Let me." She took the tray from him as he made a big show of kissing her cheek.

Anne went over to the staircase leading down onto a flagstone patio. Duke followed. As Anne put her foot on the first step, she felt a bump from behind. With her hands on the tray, she couldn't grab the handrail to stop her fall. She tumbled down the stairs, landing hard on the flagstone. For most people, the fall would have been inconsequential. But for Anne, it meant the end of her pregnancy. It also led to the discovery that she had a septate uterus. With her marriage already struggling, it had meant her chance for motherhood was slim.

After returning to D.C., Duke had milked the sympathy card for months. His approval ratings grew daily. But in private, a chill had settled between them.

"I've been talking to Senator Roberts. He tells me that children are critical to showing you're a good family man. They make the public relate to you. We're going to have to figure this out."

To Duke, children were simply chess pieces to use as strategy to gain what you want. Since she could no longer give him children, the news of his affair came as no surprise. After months of litigation, Duke made her an offer. If she would sign a non-disclosure agreement and agree to a closed divorce settlement, everything regarding her books and the farm would be hers. After a year of lawyers, she was tired. She agreed.

Sadly, in the end, Anne still had had to sell her beloved farm.

From that moment on she had stopped living. She existed in a bubble. Months crept by. A year went past. Then another. Then one day she'd stumbled across an advertisement for an old decrepit Victorian in Colorado. When she'd arrived in Carolan Springs, she felt as if she had found her home.

Life had given her a second chance.

Now it had all come back to haunt her once again.

As the sobs racked her, the reminder of what she had lost filled her with agony. The new Mrs. Freemont would give Duke the needed boost at the polls with her pregnancy.

The sobs grew stronger and stronger. All the emotions that she had held back so long sought escape. Grief came in waves. Loss of her marriage. Loss of a chance at motherhood. Loss of self.

Kandi's words came to her mind. "You hate men." No, she didn't hate *men*. She had hated one man. One man who had taken everything from her. But no more.

All this time she had thought she had healed. That she had made peace with everything that had happened. But she bore the burden of it. She hadn't been at fault because she couldn't bear a child. No, Duke lusted for power and he would do anything to attain it. She had to let go. She had to release any remaining power he held over her.

"I forgive you." With those simple words, shackles she had placed on her heart lifted. She pressed her hands over her eyes and took in deep cleansing breaths.

Chapter Thirteen

A knock on the truck's passenger window startled Anne. Sheriff Carson. She had been so deep within her own suffering and past memories that she hadn't heard the vehicle pull up. Anne ran the window down.

"Everything okay here?" He laid his hand on the door jamb. His Stetson shielded his face.

"Yes. I'm fine." She rubbed her eyes, sniffed, and hoped her face wasn't covered in snot.

He glanced down the road. "Not good to sit on the side here. Too many cars come around that curve pretty fast."

"Sorry. I just pulled over for a minute." Anne caught her reflection in the side mirror. Thankfully, no snot.

"Well, it's easy for someone to back-end you before you know it. It's best if you prevent it from happening in the future."

Her brow furrowed as she looked at him. Was he talking about being parked here or the fiasco that had just occurred? Had he been there?

Anne pushed her bangs back. "Okay. Thanks. I'm leaving now."

"You sure you're okay to drive?" His eyebrows rose with the question.

"Yes. I'm fine. In fact, I'm much better now."

"You take care, then." He tipped his hat and took a few steps away from the vehicle.

Anne pulled off the shoulder and onto the pavement. She glanced in the rearview mirror. Carson stood next to his cruiser, staring after her.

As she drove, Anne made a commitment. She hadn't come this far not to get what she wanted. She remembered a quote and repeated it aloud: "'I can and I will'—and no one is going to stop me from making a new life here."

She cranked up the radio. An upbeat tune came through the speakers. She sang loudly and out of tune to its lyrics. Anne steered the vehicle toward the hospital.

She pulled into the parking lot. Grabbing some tissues from the console, she checked her reflection.

In the hospital, she made a beeline for the bathroom. Anne stared at a fragile-looking woman in the long wall of mirrors. Her eyes were puffy and red and her face blotched from crying.

After washing her hands, she used a towel to pat her face with cold water. The scratchy brown towel only made her face redder. Anne grabbed the only makeup in her purse, a beeswax lip stain. She applied it quickly with a deft hand. Now her entire face looked red. She stuck out her tongue at the mirror image just as another lady entered the bathroom.

"I feel ya, honey. I have a lot of those days too." The woman headed to the end stall.

Anne chuckled to herself as she left the room. She strode over to the reception desk. A young nurse sat there.

Anne smiled. "Good morning. Is Eliza de French still in room 102?"

The nurse turned her gaze to the computer monitor. A few clicks on her keyboard later, she replied, "No. She's been moved to the upper level. Room 204."

"Thanks." Anne took the stairs to the next floor.

Finding Eliza's room, she saw the statuesque woman sitting up in bed. The bright white bandage on her head contrasted with her ebony straightened hair.

Eliza smiled as she entered. "Anne. So very nice of you to come."

"I'm sorry it wasn't sooner." She set her purse down on a chair.

"I can certainly understand." She pointed to the town's paper lying beside her on the bed. "And it can possibly account for what I see before me. I'm sorry you're going through this ordeal."

"Well, my secret's out." Anne stood next to the bed.

Eliza sighed. "We all have our secrets."

"But 'my ordeal' is nothing compared to what you've experienced. Here, I brought you this. I hope you like it. I've been experimenting with this winter cream." Anne handed Eliza the container holding the lotion.

Eliza opened it. "Thank you. I've wanted my gloves, but every time I put them on my hands, they ask me to remove them." She unscrewed the jar top and breathed in the lavender fragrance. "Divine." She applied it to her hands. "This lotion is simply wonderful. And you make it?"

"Yes. I've always enjoying making my own personal products. And lately I've had a hard time sleeping, so I made up a batch. Hope provided the lavender essential oil."

"Wonderful." Eliza sighed.

"It's good to see you feeling better. What do the doctors say?"

"I'm going to be fine, though I had a pretty good concussion from hitting the window. I've had some awful headaches, but they say that's normal as the brain heals and repairs." She closed her eyes for a moment. "Strangely enough, I've been sleeping much better. No need to take the sleep aids anymore."

"They always say you can find something good in any situation if you look hard enough." Anne pulled the chair over next to the bed.

Eliza leaned back on the bed.

"Here let me help you." Anne fluffed the pillows beneath Eliza. The gaunt woman cautiously turned over on her side. Her face became serious and her voice lower. "Keep reaching out to Kandi. She's hurt, but she'll come around."

Anne sat and looked down at her hands. "I just wanted to start over. I wasn't trying to hide anything. In a way, I'm rediscovering who I am. I would have told her eventually."

"You need not explain anything to me. I understand the desire to be in a place of security. Of allowing time to heal." She sighed deeply once more.

"Eliza—"

Eliza held her hand up to stop Anne. "I know what you're going to say. What am I, a black woman that stands out against a sea of white faces, doing in Carolan Springs?"

Anne laughed. "Well, actually, I was going to ask about your fan club." She waved toward the display of numerous expensive flower arrangements. "But since you brought it up, you're right. I am nosy. From what I can gather, the town is middle to lower income. We have some wealthy residents, but not many gorgeous African-American supermodels. So, yes, I'm curious as to what brought you here."

"While I appreciate your compliment, beauty can also be detrimental." Sadness passed across Eliza's face before she continued. "Years ago, I came to Colorado for a photo shoot. After we were done, I decided to explore on my own. I rented a car and took off for a drive. Unfortunately, or fortunately, depending on how you look at it, I wasn't used to driving in the mountains.

Eliza poured some water from a plastic container and took a sip of water before speaking. "I did what most people do. I rode the brakes down the mountain and next thing I knew—no brakes. Luckily, I was able to coast into town. As you know, Carolan Springs isn't a big town, so it had only a few vehicles for rent and those were gone. The wrong parts were sent for my car. I ended up staying the entire week.

"I met Kandi the first day." Eliza stopped speaking and a strange look passed over her face. She quickly took another sip of water. Now composed again, she continued. "Kandi's the one who got me a room at Marla's Bed and Breakfast."

"Wait. I thought Marla was the reporter."

"She is but being a reporter here is only a part-time job." Eliza moved into a different position.

"Sorry, please continue your story," Anne replied.

"Well, Kandi took me out for a hike to a beautiful lake. As we made our way around the lake, we came across a cabin that was up for sale. Everyone had been so kind and friendly. I knew I wanted to return, so I bought the place. Just like that.

"Now I come here when I don't need to be in New York or LA, or on location. It took some time for everyone to get used to me, but now I am acquainted with quite a few of the town's residents. They've accepted me, and I've accepted them." She rubbed her head, and a furrow appeared between her eyes.

"Oh, I'm so sorry." Anne stood up. "I should let you rest. Need anything before I go?"

"No, thank you." Eliza grimaced.

As if by telepathy, a nurse appeared. "Time for your medication."

Eliza held out her hand and Anne took it. "Thank you again for coming. I appreciate it very much. Please give my regards to Kandi."

"I will." She gave Eliza's hand a little squeeze. Anne determined she would see Kandi if she had to camp out on the young woman's porch.

Chapter Fourteen

Anne drove directly to Kandi's and marched up to the kitchen door.

She knocked.

No answer.

She waited.

"Kandi, I know you're in there. Open this door!" Anne banged again. "I'm not leaving until you open this door, young lady. You need me, you know. Who else is going to help you find the killer?"

"Hey, there." A woman's voice interrupted her rant.

Anne turned to see a group of people coming from the direction of her house.

Someone in the crowd spoke. "We were just going over to see you."

"You were?" Anne let her hand drop to her side.

The crowd parted.

"Yes." Kandi stood with her hands clutched in front of her. "Everyone has shared how this is a great opportunity for our homesteading fair. We have a famous author in our midst. We'd...I'd...like to ask if you will be the headliner of the fair."

All eyes were on her.

Anne hated the idea of headlining the fair, but knew she had no choice if she were going to make it up to Kandi. "Of course."

Everyone cheered.

"Great." A woman's voice carried from the back of the group. "Let's get planning."

The elderly man from the last disastrous meeting spoke. "Is there coffee? I'm cold."

"Yes, Mr. Culpepper." Kandi pointed to the house. "I also have some items for sandwiches, along with some pickled eggs, potato salad, and some blueberry crumble with fresh cream."

He licked his lips. "Well, then. What are we doing standing around out here for? Let's get to work." He rubbed his hands together and strode forward.

Everyone followed after him, leaving Kandi and Anne alone. Both had hung back as the group entered the house.

Anne reached over and laid her hand on Kandi's arm. "I'm sorry, Kandi. Sincerely. I did not mean to be secretive. I simply wanted some space."

"I still feel like such a fool. I can't believe I didn't recognize you." Kandi wrung her hands together. "You really hurt me by not trusting me."

"It's not surprising at all. I have a totally different hair color and hairstyle, removed the entire makeup mask, and gained about forty pounds. You'd be surprised at what good makeup and lighting can do for you." She grinned.

Kandi glanced up at Anne. "You know in some ways,

I'm really excited. This is going to be such a great thing for our community. In other ways, I want to stay mad at you." She crossed her arms over her chest.

"Truce, then?" Anne held out her hand.

Kandi caught her hand and pulled her into a hug. "I don't want to stay mad—"

"Hey, come on. I got me some things to be doing." A man's voice interrupted the scene.

The two women laughed as Mr. Culpepper threw his hands in the air before being admonished to come back inside by his wife.

"Come on, you." Anne linked her arm with Kandi's.

"Forty pounds, huh?" Kandi winked at Anne, who swatted at the young woman. Kandi laughed and went on, "After the entire thing with poor Rusty, we decided to focus on poultry as our primary theme. Workshops early in the day will be about chicks and brooders, then on to pullets, and finally on to the hens. In the evening we're going to have a 'rooster' themed dance."

Anne's eyebrows rose.

"I know…I know what you're thinking. It's a bit hokey. But I think it fits us." Kandi pushed her hair behind her ears.

Anne replied. "Agree. I think it will be fun. And I like hokey. What else do we need to talk about?"

"You'll have two presentations. One in the morning and one in the afternoon. Even without any of the main items, I'm hearing rooms are booking up quickly. Having your name added as speaker is going to be a big draw. Thanks again for doing this. You're the best."

"Egg-xactly," Anne chimed in.

Kandi groaned. "Oh no. Not you too! I've had to deal with those kinds of puns for, *like*, weeks from Stanley."

"Then it's my pleasure to continue the hokey pun-fest. I'm egg-static to be part of a successful hokey homestead fair."

Kandi groaned. Then they both burst out laughing.

Before Anne knew it, the fair was upon them. The town was decked out in all its finery promoting the fair. Stores were packed with day tourists and cafes with those staying at local bed and breakfasts. Sam had rented out his place on HomeAway and two couples from Texas were staying there.

Although Anne was used to speaking in front of audiences, this would be her biggest live audience. She launched into the advantages and benefits of backyard chickens. There were many beginners interested in chickens so lots of hands shot up in the air with questions.

"I only have a very small yard. It's just me and my husband. Can I get just one chicken?"

"I don't recommend it. Chicken are social creatures. They're a bit like teenagers. They need others around and they'll definitely have a pecking order. If you don't have the space, try a bantam or smaller chicken breed. You could easily have three to five hens. And trust me, you'll have friends that want any extra eggs you might have!"

Anne pointed at a woman wearing a baby snuggly in her Tula wrap.

"I'd only seen white and brown eggs at my grocery store. But earlier today I saw some blue ones, some pink, and even some green eggs. How do you get those kinds of eggs and do they taste different than a white egg?"

Anne moved to the side of the stage where a dozen eggs were in a clear container. "Each of these eggs is a different color. Some"—she held up one—"even have spots on them. This is determined by the type of hens you have. For instance, if you want a brown egg, then your best choices would be something like a Rhode Island Red, a Wyandotte, an Astralorp, or Orpington.

Ameraucana or Aracaunas, or what some refer to as Easter-eggers, lay blue or green eggs."

A small hand shot up.

"Yes? You in the back." She motioned to the small boy.

"Um, uh, how do you know if the eggs are good for you? I mean, you know, like, okay to eat? I mean, when you go to the store, you can trust they're okay."

"Good question. Thanks for asking." The boy beamed at the praise.

"First, let's start with the timing. When you go outside and retrieve eggs on a daily basis, those eggs are fresh. Eggs in the store can have taken up to five weeks just to get on your refrigerator shelf."

Some people in the crowd gasped, and Anne heard, "Is that true?"

"It's true. Look it up." She smiled at the crowd.

"Healthy egg yolks will look like a bright orange sun and will be firm and not break. Eggs from your backyard chickens are often healthier for you with less cholesterol and saturated fat, yet have more vitamins A and E, omega 3s, and beta carotene. Just one more reason to consider getting some of your own hens.

"Also, remember, chickens aren't vegetarian. They're omnivores. They love bugs. They need protein. One of the best things you can give your girls are mealworms. They love them."

A little girl on the front row said loudly, "I don't want to eat worms."

The audience roared. Definitely a good sign when people enjoyed themselves. Anne spied Kandi signaling for her to conclude. "Okay, time for one last question."

"I bought some chickens, and I think they're dying. They started losing all their feathers. They look horrible." The woman grimaced. "Should I ask for my money back?"

"They're molting. Now that the weather is cooler, they're getting ready to put on their winter coats. In a few weeks, you'll be thinking you have the prettiest chickens in town."

Anne smiled at the crowd. "Thank you everyone. You've been great. I'll be over at the table in booth forty-five, if you'd like to stop by."

The audience clapped, and Anne left the stage. As she moved to the right on the stairs, a group of folk musicians climbed to set up for their performance at lunch.

Anne met Kandi. "How's it going? I tried to say hi this morning, but you were—"

"Running around like a chicken with my head cut off?" Kandi tossed her head, her ponytail bouncing. "It's been crazy. I think we, *like*, doubled our numbers from last year. And it's all due to you. You've made this a huge success." She hugged Anne who returned the hug.

Anne smiled as she grasped Kandi's arms. "Don't count yourself short. Your hokey idea looks to have struck a chord with a lot of folks. People interested in homesteading can learn while others can simply enjoy the fair and take home some of Sally's homemade peach jam."

"It's, *like*, the best isn't it?" Kandi smiled. "I have her saving me a couple jars."

"Me too. Plus the vendor booths, the petting farm, the music performances, and the rooster dance are all great ideas."

"Have to give credit where credit is due. I had some initial ideas, but when everything went nuts after Ralph died, believe it or not, Stanley stepped in and took over. I guess that old drill sergeant instinct kicked in. He had everyone working on a section of the fair. And, *like*, he told me, they all attacked it to win the war. He *persuaded*"—she made quotes in the air with her fingers—"a bunch of the local store owners to, *like*, pony up money. He told them how their businesses would benefit, and *voilà*, there you go. Done deal. I'm super stoked." Kandi's phone dinged with a text. "Oops. Meltdown at the kid's petting area. Gotta go." She hurried off.

"Hi." A deep voice came from behind her.

Anne turned to find Sheriff Carson standing there. His six foot four height was imposing and his broad shoulders blocked some of the sun.

"Hello." She reached up and subconsciously smoothed her hair.

"Good job up there." He nodded toward the stage. "Walk with me?"

"Well, I was going to head over to the food tent."

"Sounds good to me. I haven't eaten all morning. May I join you?"

"You off duty?" She peered up at him. Short black curls peeked from the back of his hat, signaling a haircut put off.

"I've been here since four this morning. Got the deputies on 'stop being a jack—'" He stumbled over his words. "Well, you can probably figure out the rest. Got some of the local veterans acting as posse on any bad behavior." He smiled down at her and she noticed one of his teeth had a small chip in the corner. It made him look less invincible.

They'd reached the food tent where all matter of intriguing and mouthwatering smells drifted in the air.

A lyrical voice called out, "Carson! Carson!" A woman hurried toward them. She wore a form-fitting burgundy and cream sweater, a pair of forest green corduroys, and tall brown boots with heels that added height to her petite frame. Instead of jarring, the burgundy made her scarlet hair glow. She was—in a word—stunning.

Anne glanced down at her wrinkled chambray shirt, jeans, and ankle boots. She wished she'd considered her outfit a bit more this morning, but five o'clock had come way too early and she'd wanted to wear something comfortable. The word *hokey* came unbidden to her mind. Just because she'd given up couture didn't mean she should give up caring at all. She smoothed her shirt with her hands.

The sheriff smiled as the woman approached. "Hi, Sorcha. What can I do for you?"

Sorcha purred. "There you are! I've been looking all over for you."

Anne took a step forward.

"Oh... hello." Sorcha turned back to Carson. "Oh, don't look so sad. You know I've got some food for you. Shepherd's pie and scotch eggs—your favorite. Come on." She hooked her arm through his, propelling him away.

"Later?" he said over his shoulder.

"Sure. No worries." She waved them off.

Who am I kidding? No way can I compete with the fiery-hot Celtic Sophia Loren.

That unbidden thought stopped her in her tracks. Compete? She didn't even feel any attraction to the man. If anything, he was condescending to her. He also seemed to always appear when she looked, or felt, at her worst. No. She didn't feel anything.

He's simply being friendly and I'm tired.

Chapter Fifteen

After giving her second talk, Anne told Kandi she was leaving for the day. One of the first things she'd fallen in love with in Carolan Springs was the wide tree-lined streets and the various shops where you could browse at leisure so she decided to stroll down Main Street. Normally quiet, the last few days they'd thrived with people from the fair. People crowded around displays put out by shop vendors and street musicians performed varying types of music. It all served to present a festive air to the city and was inviting her to participate.

Fall was certainly in the air. Leaves tickled by the wind provided windswept colors on the swept sidewalk in front of her and the aspens quivered and rustled as she enjoyed their golden dance in the sun. The remnants of melting snow were the only reminder of the storm from last night. Anne marveled at how quickly the weather could change in Colorado.

After browsing in a few shops, Anne reached the town bookstore. All of her homesteading books now graced the shop's window. Taking a step back, she turned to move down the street when the store's door flew open. A pretty, young woman ran out of the door. "Hello. Aren't you Ms. Tenet? I mean, Ms. Freemont?"

"Yes." Anne smiled back.

"How do you like the display?" the young woman asked excitedly.

She inspected it alongside the woman. The display spotlighted a backdrop of a farm scene that featured rustic folk art chickens along with a milk jug brimming with artificial sunflowers. From the ceiling, bees with gossamer wings flew in front of the artificial sky. Anne's books were stacked or opened to showcase photos.

"It's very nice. Did you create it?" Anne complimented the woman with reddish gold hair and green eyes. Freckles liberally dotted her nose.

"Yes, I did." She smiled brightly, revealing a set of white teeth encased in braces. "Oh, and I'm Missy."

"Would you like me to sign some of the books, Missy?"

"Really?" Missy squealed and jumped up and down before composing herself. "Oh, that would be wonderful!"

She opened the door and escorted Anne into the shop. Inside, the smell of old books mingled with the scent of chocolate chip cookies. A woman appeared in the doorway. Anne's breath caught in her throat. It was Sorcha.

Where the girl was cute and pretty, the woman was beautiful. Her mahogany locks which had cascaded in waves over her shoulders were now pulled back with a clip and she'd traded her high-heeled brown boots for some burgundy velvet flats.

"Mom, this is Anne Freemont!" Missy's huge grin barely contained her noticeable excitement.

"Yes, I believe that's true." She turned to Anne. "I'm sorry I was so abrupt earlier. I knew I had a short time for lunch before I had to get back here. I'm Sorcha." She smiled and held out her hand which Anne took.

Anne returned the smile. "No worries. I know today was hectic for everyone."

Sorcha released Anne's hand and pointed to the window. "I hope you approve of the display."

"I do. I was just telling..."

"Missy," the girl interjected.

"I was just telling Missy that I would be happy to sign some of the books for you."

"Wonderful." The woman motioned toward a small alcove Anne hadn't noticed on entering the shop. "Please, take a seat."

A lit fire crackled and warmed the tiny room. Missy turned on a few floor lamps, dispelling any lingering shadows. Anne quickly scanned the room and headed toward an overstuffed chair next to the fireplace. Draped over every chair was a soft throw in various jewel tones. She spied a pair of closed heavy wooden doors. Across the top on the door's fascia, a carved wooden sign spelled out *Library*.

Anne sighed deeply. "This is wonderful."

"Thank you. It's my favorite room in the shop." The woman closed the doors behind them.

Sorcha pulled stacks of Anne's books from a couple of the boxes. She and Anne set the books on a mahogany pie crust table in the adjoining room.

She motioned to the chair that Missy had pulled up to a larger table against the wall. As she sunk into the comfortable high-back chair, a plate holding a sweet-smelling cookie was placed in front of her.

"I'll be back in a minute." The woman left and returned shortly bearing a tea pot and two glasses of milk.

"If you're like me, you'll want milk with your cookies and hot tea too." She set the items on the table. "Sorcha is a beautiful and unique name. Is that Irish?"

The woman threw back her head and laughed heartily. "Oh, no. Good thing my *mathair*—mother—didn't hear you say that. Celtic—Scottish. It means bright, radiant. As you can imagine from seeing my daughter, I too came into this world with bright red hair."

The woman took a sip of her tea. "My great-grandfather came to Colorado during the gold rush. He met my grandmother and never left." She focused intently on Anne. Her green eyes were rimmed with brown eyeliner and almost glowed like a cat's. "I heard that you are helping Kandi with her dilemma."

"Her dilemma?" Anne took another bite of cookie, the warm chocolate infusing her mouth with its sweetness. "Oh. Well, I don't believe for one moment Kandi killed Ralph, if that's what you mean."

Sorcha fixed her piercing gaze on Anne from across the table. "Yes, it's what I mean."

Anne squirmed under the intense appraisal. "I'm not sure how I can help her, but I'm doing what I can."

Sorcha sipped her tea.

Maybe Sorcha could give Anne some insights. "What

about Ralph? Did he have any enemies or anyone with a grudge—?"

"No. Of course not." She cocked an eyebrow. "Are you referring to Hope?"

Anne nodded, sadly wiping her chocolate-covered fingers on a napkin instead of popping them in her mouth.

"Such a heartbreaking story." Sorcha took in a deep breath. "Faith and Ralph fell in love in high school. Families in this town have lived here since the town's inception. I believe Faith's ancestry relates to Romanian gypsies. But everyone in town considered her relations witches. And there'd always been bad blood between the two clans."

She frowned and shook her head. "Anyway, his parents were dead set against the union. When he'd come home from college they could see that his relationship with Faith was becoming serious. So they contacted an old friend in another state and got Ralph an internship. It made sure he couldn't visit with Faith. Yet, what Ralph didn't know at the time was that his father was intercepting all communication."

"That's horrible!" Anne's cup rattled as she set it in the saucer.

Sorcha nodded affirmation. "No one has proof but his dad, who was mayor at the time, may have paid off the postman to intercept all of Ralph's letters to Faith." When she saw Anne's surprised look, she acknowledged it. "Remember, the prejudice ran deep back then against Faith's people. They were tolerated but the idea of a marriage was out of the question. As powerful as

Ralph's father was, it would have been pretty easy to pay someone to look the other way."

Anne motioned Sorcha to continue with the painful story. "Since Ralph thought Faith had never written back, he believed she was over him. He met his wife in college. She came from a wealthy family. They got married during his senior year. But what was most heartbreaking was that Ralph didn't know Faith had gotten pregnant with Hope on his last visit back to the Springs."

Sorcha took a sip of tea, leaving a smear of coral lipstick on the rim. "Of course, Faith thought he had simply stolen a treasure and left. She felt he had used her. She was crushed."

She took a sip of the milk. "Then Faith refused to tell anyone who the father was."

"Please continue," Anne urged. Maybe this story could reveal a clue.

"Ralph didn't live here… or even visit for that matter. Whenever he'd say something about coming home, his folks would always say the timing was off. His parents would always go to visit them. It's sad but I think they knew that Hope was Ralph's.

"Years passed. Ralph and his family were in a terrible car accident. His wife and teenage son were killed. Ralph was hurt pretty badly and had to go through months of rehabilitation. His parents urged him to move home so they could care for him. I guess they figured it had been long enough.

"But as soon as Ralph saw Hope, he knew. He tried to reconcile with Faith, but she wouldn't have anything to do with him. She thought he had abandoned her. Faith finally did confess to him that Hope was his daughter. She asked him why he hadn't responded to her letters." Sorcha leaned back in her chair before continuing.

"By that time, Hope had left to go to medical school. She thought she'd received a full ride scholarship, but Ralph paid for every bit of it."

Anne shook her head at the injustice done on the young couple. "Wow. That's some story. How do you know all this?"

Sorcha stared pointedly at Anne. "Sometimes all you have to do is take the pieces and pull them together." She picked up a tapestry throw on the chair next to her. She turned it over and showed it to Anne. "On this side, all you see are the threads of varying colors, but when you turn it over, the pattern becomes clear. Or"—her smile widened—"basically, wait to find out from the town's gossip grapevine." She set the tapestry down and continued.

"Ralph begged Faith to marry him. She refused. He tried to provide support, but she refused that as well. She also forbid him telling Hope that he was her father. Faith did finally relent just a few years ago and told Hope. Then Faith started exhibiting early signs of dementia. So Hope moved back to care for her mother."

She paused. "But old hurts run deep. Poor Hope will never get the chance now to have a relationship with her father."

"You're right. That's just so sad." Anne sat back in her chair. "So Faith never married?"

"No." Sorcha's voice broke. "And he loved her until the very end."

Anne glanced down at her now-empty plate. What would it be like to have one person love you for so long and so deeply? How cruel Ralph's father had been.

Sorcha placed another cookie on Anne's plate. "Please, have another one. If not, then I'll end up eating them all."

Missy peeked her head around the corner and Anne finished the cookie quickly. While she went to the bathroom to wash her hands, the tea items were removed, the table cleaned, and a pen provided. Anne signed the books placed in front of her, with Missy affixing *signed copy* stickers.

Anne closed the last book. "I really appreciate your display and having my books on hand. Honestly, a bit surprising to see you have so many."

"I ordered in for the homesteading fair. I'm hoping to sell these and then take orders for the town now that we have an author in our midst." She winked.

Anne rose. "Thank you again for the cookies and conversation. It was nice visiting with you, Sorcha. Missy, thank you for all your hard work on the display." The girl beamed with the praise.

Sorcha patted the stack of books. "Thank you for signing these. Please stop in again. I normally try to make cookies when one of the book clubs in town is meeting."

Anne thanked the woman and exited the shop. The bell over the door jangled behind her as she hunched her shoulders and headed home. Thoughts swirled in her mind.

The story of Ralph's and Hope's lives had certainly

been a tragedy. Had Faith ever told Hope that Ralph paid her way through college? Or had she kept that fact to herself? Had Hope finally taken her revenge on Ralph for neglecting her and her mother all those years? But then, why wait? Hope had been back for more than five years. Why now?

Chapter Sixteen

A few days after the fair had concluded, Anne went to Kandi's for a visit where the conversation soon turned to Ralph's murder.

"So, any news?" Anne scraped a plate into Kandi's compost bucket and closed the lid.

"My lawyer says it's going to be a tough fight. It looks like Ralph definitely died from an axe blow. My fingerprints are on the handle and it was found in my yard. Plus, my DNA is *everywhere*. My attorney says we have to create reasonable doubt in the jury's mind."

Tears pooled in her eyes. "I don't think I'll be able to survive in prison. I didn't do it. Why would I kill Ralph?"

A knot formed in Anne's throat at seeing Kandi in such pain. She needed to provide a distraction and offer some hope. "Who else may have had it in for Ralph? Can you think of anything, no matter how small, that could lead to a clue?"

"I've been wracking my brain, but I can't come up with anything." Kandi wiped her eyes, which now shone with renewed determination.

"We just need that one clue that helps us figure

everything out. So no giving up, okay?" Anne squeezed the girl's hand.

Kandi groaned. "Well, it better be fast. My initial court appearance is next month."

Once they'd finishing cleaning up, Anne said goodnight and headed home. She walked to the hedge that divided her yard from Ralph's. The crime scene tape had been removed, and she stared at the area where Ralph's body had been found.

What had happened here? Did Ralph know his killer? What were they doing out in the backyard? Was the axe the intentional murder weapon or a weapon of opportunity?

Stewart stood the most to gain from his uncle's death, but she didn't rule out Jeff and his devious nature. Hope might have been hurt by the man she'd found out was her father, but was it enough to want to kill him? Hope seemed to be successful and financially secure, but she'd said herself that Ralph's money would really help with Faith's care. Faith was certainly too frail to harm Ralph, and why would she want to do so now, after all this time? Was she upset Ralph hadn't cared for her and the baby? Most of the possible suspects claimed to have been sleeping at the time of the attack, but that didn't mean anything. It's not like the killer was going to admit to having been there that night.

What am I missing?

A hand latched onto her arm.

She screamed.

"Hey! Settle down." Sam laughed. "It's just me."

"Are you crazy?" She punched him on the arm and pulled free. "You scared me to death."

"What are you doing? Probably not good to be wandering around back here. You know what they say about the killer returning …wait, a minute." He cocked an eyebrow and grinned at her.

"Ha. Ha. Very funny. Not! Stewart beat you to that old saying. I'm trying to help Kandi. I wanted to see if I could think of anything."

"You need to leave it to the sheriff's office." His tone had become serious.

"Did someone mention the sheriff?" Anne and Sam turned to see Carson standing in a clump of trees.

"Are you *spying* on me?" Anne's voice rose.

"I'm spying—as you put it—on anyone who comes into this yard. It's called investigative work. I actually wanted to check out this property boundary again to confirm if anyone entered or exited this way."

Anne hadn't thought of that. The edges of the property bordered a forested area with a seasonal creek running through it. The town had wanted to preserve the green space, so they'd created a creek-side path for bikers, runners, and walkers.

Had the killer crept up from the stream, killed Ralph, and then returned the same way?

Anne shivered. The trail also wound around her property. She looked beyond the hedge to the woods, dark and menacing. Was a serial killer on the loose and she the next victim? Her mind raced with new possibilities and threats. Anne jumped when she turned back and found Carson had walked up next to them.

His face hardened as he glanced down at her. "This is a formal investigation. Do not, I repeat, *do not* insert yourself into something you will regret." He didn't wait for a reply, but strode back toward the forest edge.

"That man is something else. Just who does he think he is, talking to me like that?" Anne bristled.

Sam laughed. "You crack me up. He *thinks* he is the law. Because—he is!" He turned toward her. "Seriously, you need to be careful. Someone murdered Ralph in cold blood. Stay out of it."

"Where were you the night of his murder?" She was shocked to hear the words leave her mouth.

He tensed. "Are you kidding me? You're asking if I murdered Ralph?"

"Well...I..." Anne fidgeted.

"You have got some nerve, lady. No wonder you needed to change your identity if that's how you treat people."

The words cut deeply. She threw her shoulders back and dared herself not to cry in front of him. They glared at one another. Finally, without a word, he turned and marched across the yard.

After Sam rounded the corner, she turned toward her house. As she did, something in the compost pile caught her eye. She glanced over at it. It was something tiny and reddish that was partially hidden under the lilac bushes. What was it?

Maybe she'd found the clue she'd been waiting to discover. She advanced toward it but stopped herself. She looked toward the forest. Carson stood there, watching.

He must have heard everything. Her cheeks reddened in embarrassment.

She glanced toward the compost pile. She'd have to come back when Dudley Do-Right wasn't on guard. If she went for the object now, he might confiscate a needed clue. Because it could be the very thing that could help Kandi, she didn't want to take the chance. And since there was no more crime scene tape, she reasoned it was fair game and she couldn't get in trouble.

Anne crossed toward the opening in the lilacs. Carson may have won that round, but it only served to make her more determined to prove Kandi's innocence.

Anne awoke to find her room bathed in bright light. She pulled back the curtain to spy a layer of white snow glistening in the sun. *Shoot.* While she'd read Colorado could be notorious for its mood swings, the timing of this snow couldn't be more frustrating. It was still September and it had already snowed twice. But this time, almost a foot of snow covered the ground and Anne had no desire to go digging in snow-covered compost it to find whatever object she'd seen. With no way to figure out where it had been, her search would amount to finding a needle in a haystack. Now whatever she'd seen by the compost pile would be covered in snow for at least a few days.

Bang.

The intrusion startled Anne. Another bang. A loose shutter upstairs?

She grabbed a wool jacket from her closet and put it on over her flannel pj's. She slid her feet out of her slippers and into some heavier rain boots she found in the mudroom. In the kitchen she looked longingly at the coffee pot, but she needed to get the shutter refastened before it broke.

Remembering the back stairwell to be dimly lit, Anne grabbed the flashlight from the side of the refrigerator. She opened the door from the kitchen and started up the wood treads, well worn by the footsteps of past residents. Anne reached the landing on the second floor and spied the hall entry door with the remnants of green baize. She'd often wondered if the original owners had come from England and determined once again to do some deeper research on the house.

Anne proceeded up a set of narrow wooden steps toward the attic. The attic revealed a web of tiny rooms. Here and there boxes coated with dust sat stacked in the corners. The boxes' owners, now long gone, must have been too tired to even check the contents before leaving.

Bang. BANG.

She moved toward the sound. Inside the room, a light snow blew in from a broken window. Frigid air enveloped the room. Anne headed over to the dirt-caked window. Using a scrap of old material from the floor, she wiped off the primary panes.

Her breath caught at the magnificent view. She could see the entire park area, the perimeter of her property, and over into Ralph's yard. She moved out of that room and went across to the far left room. Here the window revealed more of the park in the distance, its trees now covered in a beautiful snow fondant. Anne could also see Kandi's house and garage area.

She squinted.

Someone moved across the yard. By the person's size and stature, it looked like Jeff. Unfortunately, it was difficult to tell for sure since he had on a heavy coat and a hat pulled low over his face. He held something in his hands. One of Kandi's chickens? But her coop was located in the other part of the yard.

The hen hung limp from the man's arm, the long neck stretched away from its body. Was the chicken's head missing? Maybe he had dispatched a chicken for dinner.

Maybe a fox or raccoon had gotten to one of the chickens, and Jeff was taking care of it before Kandi saw the damage. He disappeared around the back of the house, and Anne stepped back from the window.

Since the shutter latch had broken, she decided to close the shutters so she could lock them. It could save some heat too. She opened the window and closed the shutters with a hook and a board that pulled them tight. Then she shut and locked the window.

She returned to the other room to close the shutters there. Glancing out the window, Anne spied the same figure heading out of Ralph's yard. This time, his hands were empty.

Maybe it wasn't Jeff. The bulky coat hid the person's

figure and he or she wore a balaclava over their face, so it could've been anyone. It certainly wasn't Kandi as the figure was too tall.

Just then the figure turned and glanced toward her house. Anne pulled back from the window.

Oh, no. The shutters. I should have left them for later. Now he'll know I saw him.

The figure shielded his eyes from the bright snow and continued to look toward her home. Anne took another step back.

Something moved behind her. A mouse shot across the floor. A guttural noise made her turn. She screamed as the cat launched off one of the boxes and chased after the mouse. As she caught her breath, she heard the sound of heavy boots pounding up the stairs.

She ran to the window.

The figure had disappeared.

Nowhere to hide.

Fear pumped through her veins.

Anne searched for some type of weapon. She found a long piece of baseboard coming apart from the wall. She pulled at it and a cluster of mice shot out.

She screamed again. Shaking, she could hear the boots running down the hall. She raised the stick of wood over her head, ready to strike.

"Whoa." Sam held up his hand. "Careful, there."

So thankful to see a friendly face, Anne broke down in tears and threw herself in his arms. Sobbing, she buried her face in his jacket. A mouse scurried past with the cat in hot pursuit and Anne yelped again, her feet dancing.

He hugged her to his side. "Hey, now, it's okay. They're

only mice. I thought someone was killing you the way you were screaming." He took her wooden weapon and threw it down on the floor, raising a cloud of dust in the air.

After Anne regained her composure, the pair made their way down the stairs. In the kitchen, Sam motioned her to sit in the chair. After he made coffee, he grabbed a nearby throw and rested it around her shoulders. Next he bent down in front of Anne and began rubbing her hands in his.

"Your hands are like ice. It's freezing up there. What were you doing in the attic on such a cold day anyway?" He didn't wait for an answer but continued, "Well, one good thing. I think your mouser is having a field day up there right now. I didn't know you had a cat."

"Kandi gave him to me."

"Sweet girl. In this old house, you're going to want a cat. The place had been empty so long that I'm sure there are quite a few nests around." He excused himself from the kitchen. When he returned, he held a bag. He extracted a bottle of brandy.

Even with the coat on, she shivered and pulled the quilt tighter. He poured some coffee and cream into a mug and added a generous capful of brandy. He handed the cup to Anne. "Here. Drink this. Old Victorian remedy for shock. It's really supposed to be in tea, but this works too."

She took a sip of the coffee. The heat trickled down her throat and the brandy created warmth in her chest. She sighed. "Sorry about that. I just thought you were—"

"Listen. I wanted to stop by and apologize. I was rude, and I shouldn't have said what I did last night." Sam scooted a chair back from the table and sat.

"Thank you. I'm sorry about it too."

"Friends again?"

"Friends." She smiled at him.

He shrugged out of his jacket and poured himself a cup of coffee sans brandy.

"No Victorian remedy for you?" she quipped.

"As much as I'd like to, I'm on duty. I keep it in my car in case I come across someone who's experienced a shock. Though you never heard me say that." He winked. "So what happened?"

"There was a shutter banging upstairs. I went up there and saw…someone in Ralph's yard. I stepped back and must have disturbed a mouse. Then the cat sprang at me from a box. It scared me so I yelled, and then you came running and I thought…" She caught herself from breaking into more sobs.

"Hey, slow down. It's okay." He stood up and grabbed his jacket off the hook. "I'm going to go take a look around. Be back in a minute."

Anne nodded. The hot coffee and brandy soothed her mind and body.

In a few minutes, Sam returned. "I went over to Ralph's and also scoped out your yard. No one there. But I did see footprints." His face turned serious. "You need to report this to the sheriff."

"Report what?" Anne set her cup on the table.

"It may have been the killer returning to the crime scene. Did you see who it was?"

"No. I couldn't tell. I don't know. I could just be imagining things with all that's been going on." She pulled the quilt tighter.

"That could be true, but you need to report it. I went ahead and radioed Carson."

"You what? I don't need—"

Her sentence was interrupted by a knock on the back door.

Sam opened the door. "Hey, Carson. That was quick." He turned to Anne. "I've got to go. I just wanted to stop by …and anyway, I'll call later." He grabbed his coat and when he did, a black balaclava fell out of the pocket.

Scooping it up, he smiled. "I'll need this on a day like today. Sheriff." With a quick wave, he left the pair.

Sheriff Carson pulled off his brown gloves. "So what seems—"

"Please take off your coat and hat. Would you like a cup of coffee?" Anne motioned to her mug.

"I've learned to never turn down a cup of coffee." He hung his Stetson on a hook and then shrugged out of his bulky jacket. As she moved to the counter, she could see that he towered above her in height. His shirt sleeves strained against his muscles, evidence of hours spent weight-lifting. Criminals would be ill-advised to try to take him on in a fight.

Anne filled a mug and sat it on the table. "Sit down. Please." He ran his fingers through his jet black hair but Anne noticed a hint of silver threads were already appearing. He took the chair facing the doors. Pulling out a pad from his pocket, he clicked a pen and began to write.

The coffee sloshed and spilled onto her jacket, reminding Anne what she wore. *Oh, geez. Does this man always have to see me looking horrible?*

She set her cup down. "If it's okay, can you excuse me for a minute?"

When he nodded his assent, she went to her room and changed into jeans and a peacock blue sweater before quickly brushing her hair and teeth. She washed her face and put on some lavender lotion. She returned to the kitchen.

Carson set down the brandy Sam had left behind. "A bit early, isn't it?" He nodded toward the brandy.

Anne bristled. *Does he think I'm a drunk?* "I'll have you know that Sam brought that in and put some in my coffee. And you know what? I'm an adult woman. If I want to drink brandy, I'll drink it anytime I damn well please." She crossed her arms over her chest.

A smirk played around his lips.

Oh, this man. Why am I even explaining anything to him?

He looked her up and down. "Yes, you're definitely an adult woman. And yes, you may drink as long as it doesn't violate the law. I just wanted to understand your capabilities on seeing someone in Ralph's yard." He took a huge swig of coffee.

Did he just check me out? No way. Seriously?

"My capabilities are fine. See?" She stood and touched her nose with the forefinger of each hand. Then she stood on one foot. She was very pleased with herself until her ankle bent and she lost her balance. Carson moved quickly before she hit the table. Cocooned in his strong arms, she managed a shaky, "I'm fine. Let me go."

He quickly set her up on her feet. He gazed down at her. Neither of them moved.

He broke the moment. "I'm going up there to get a glimpse of what you think you saw."

"I'm coming too! And it wasn't what I think I saw. I saw him!" Anne ran and grabbed the coat from her bed.

"Okay, but you stay out of my way," he yelled down the stairs.

"I'll not be ordered around in my own home," she retorted. She rushed up the stairs and they climbed to the attic. They entered the room where she'd seen the person in Ralph's yard.

"I was closing up the shutters in this room when this all began."

As they moved closer to the windows, the kitten jumped from an adjacent box and dropped a mouse at Anne's feet. She then noticed a bunch of dead mice in a pile in the corner.

"Gross," she moaned.

The police chief reached down and picked up the cat, which immediately started purring. "Good cat." He turned to Anne. "What's its name?"

"Mouser" came out of her mouth before she thought about it.

"Well, he's certainly that." Carson stroked the cat's fur with his left hand. Anne noticed a faint band of white against the tanned skin.

Not married. Divorced probably, and no wonder. The man is infuriating!

He set the cat down and strode purposefully to the window.

"Wow. Some view from up here."

She joined him. "Yes. It's really nice."

"So where did you see the unsub?"

"Unsub?" Anne repeated.

He looked down at her. "Unidentified subject."

She pointed to Ralph's yard. He bent closer and glanced out the window.

"Okay. I'm going to make some notes and then let's get back down to the kitchen where it's warmer."

As he wrote, Anne opened the box closest to her. Bits and pieces from a teenager's room from days past. Some records, posters, a bunch of costume jewelry, and old tie-dyed tees and jeans. Tentatively, she reached inside. Anne pulled out a book from the Nancy Drew series. She held it up. From behind, she heard him chuckle.

"What else? *The Secret in the Old Attic*."

Clutching it in her hand, she moved past him and down the stairs to the kitchen.

Back downstairs, Carson held his notepad. "Anything else you want to tell me?"

Should I tell him about Jeff? Or was it Jeff? What about the dead chicken? That could mean nothing. No. Better to talk with Kandi first.

"Nope. That's everything."

He stared at her for a long time. His piercing gaze and midnight blue eyes probably made many people confess to crimes they hadn't committed. He knew she was holding something back. Finally, she broke eye contact and pretended to inspect the book she'd found.

"Okay. You think of anything else you want to tell me, let me know." He pushed his arms into the sleeves of his heavy coat and placed his hat on his head. "Thanks for the coffee."

As she let him out the front door, he left a strange absence in his wake.

She cleaned up the coffee cups and thought about her next steps. She needed to speak to Kandi. From her window, she saw someone headed up her back porch. A frantic Hope knocked on the door and didn't wait for Anne to speak. "It's Mom. I can't find her. I was at Kandi's going over the fair proceeds and she must have slipped out. She doesn't have a coat on. Please, I need some help to search for her."

"Of course, I'll help. Back in jiff." Anne swung a scarf over her coat, ran to the mudroom, and unearthed a hat and gloves.

They hurried out to the yard and set off toward the forest. Hope pointed. "I saw some tracks going this way, but since it's still snowing, they're being covered so fast."

Yelling for Faith as they moved, their voices echoed across the yards. Even with the light snow, the exertion brought sweat to Anne's brow and her sweater stuck to her back.

"Hope, I think we need more help. Let's get more people involved in the search."

The usually cheerful woman nodded solemnly. They headed back up from the creek path. The women spotted a light glowing in Ralph's kitchen. Moving up onto the porch, Anne glanced through the windows and saw Faith sitting at the table drinking from a cup.

Hope gasped and pushed through the door. Her mother smiled. "Hello. Do I know you? I'm cold. Can you start a fire for me?"

Hope removed her coat and placed it over her mother's shoulders.

"I tried to get Ralph to do it, but he won't answer me. I keep waiting, but he hasn't come yet. He's going to marry me, you know. He said so." The old woman pulled at Hope's hands. "Will you help me?"

"Of course, Mama. I'll help you." Hope patted her mother's hands.

They gathered the frail woman between them and walked to the front door. Hope ran across to Kandi's to retrieve her car, and Anne helped place Faith in the car. Pushing her felt hat back low over her ears and pulling her coat collar up, Anne hurried back inside Ralph's house. She locked the front door and turned to depart out the back.

As she walked down the hall and past the cased opening to the dining room, a figure burst from the room and grabbed onto her coat. In her attempt to get away, the pair fell in a heap to the floor. She hit out at her masked attacker, but Anne was no match for his strength. Fear pumped through her. She struggled to crawl away toward the living room.

He grabbed her. The man grunted, "You're not getting away."

Chapter Seventeen

Anne kicked and punched in a desperate attempt to free herself.

"I have you now," the man in the ski mask growled. He pushed her down on her back.

Her hands flailed out, searching. Her hand landed on a piece of firewood. Anne screamed loudly and with all the strength she could muster, brought the wood down on her attacker's head.

As the man fell, Anne pushed him away. She struggled to her feet. Moving away from her attacker, she pulled her shaking body to a standing position.

The man tried to rise.

Anne picked up another piece of wood. She clutched it in both hands, swaying back and forth. "Don't move!" She held it up over her head, readying for another attack.

A banging on the front door caught her attention. Holding the wood like a sword Anne backed out of the room. Kandi, Jeff, and a few of the other neighbors stood at the front door. Kandi spoke, "We were outside shoveling snow and heard screaming. What's happening?"

"I was attacked. I think I caught the killer." She motioned into the living room. Jeff peered around the doorjamb, while the others hung back. Curiosity seekers, though Anne could see that one person had pulled out their phone, hopefully calling 9-1-1.

Jeff entered the hallway and stood facing the man. With a quick jerk, he yanked the ski mask off.

Stewart!

He moaned and put his hand back up to his head. When Stewart pulled his hand away, his fingers were smeared in red.

A familiar deep voice carried from the front porch. "Step aside. Let me through." Sheriff Carson strode inside. Anne still clutched the wood over Stewart, who held a hand to his head.

"Busy morning?" Carson said to her. "I'll take that." He motioned for her to give him the wood. She handed it over and he set it next to the door jamb inside the room.

Stewart dragged himself over to the sofa and rested against the front. "I want her arrested! She assaulted me."

Anne bristled. "I assaulted *you*? You came after me."

Carson interrupted. "Okay, let's calm down. I'll listen to both sides." He motioned for the others to go outside and give their statements to the attending officer. Returning his attention to the pair, he nodded "Let's start with you, Stewart."

"I found *that woman*—he pointed at Anne—inside my uncle's house. I went to grab her and she attacked me."

"See, he admits to grabbing me." She ignored Carson's

motion to be quiet. "Plus, why are you wearing a ski mask, Stewart?"

"I'll ask the questions, Ms. Freemont." The sheriff motioned for Stewart to carry on.

"I was cross-country skiing on the park trail. I got up to my uncle's property and thought I saw movement in the house. I know some teens have been inside in the past. They left a mess. I wanted to catch them before they ruined anything else. I took off my skis and crept in through the kitchen."

The sheriff spoke to the deputy and lieutenant that had joined them. "Go check out the path and see if you can find those skis."

Anne opened her mouth to speak, but Carson held up his gloved hand in a stop motion. He turned to Stewart. "Continue."

"Then I got to thinking. Maybe the killer had come back, or someone was trying to rob my uncle's place. Once inside, I saw a figure in the hallway. Looked like a teen boy."

Anne harrumphed. A teen boy? Really?

Stewart pointed. "She was at the front door. Hat pulled down over their eyes, coat pulled up. Suspicious, for sure. I went around through the dining room and came up behind them. That's when he—she—started back toward the kitchen, and I grabbed her."

"See, see. He admits it. He grabbed me!" Anne raised her hands in triumph.

"Yes, I grabbed you, but then you went all nuts and started attacking me. Then she caused me to fall—"

"You caused *me* to fall!" She stamped her foot.

"Ms. Freemont." The chief pointed to a chair. "Sit." After Anne took a seat, Carson spoke. "You will get your turn. But for now you will remain silent. Am I clear?" After a stern look from him, Anne crossed her arms and clenched her lips tightly together.

Carson motioned to Stewart. "Continue."

"Um...so next thing I know, I'm being kicked and bitten, so I tried to get on top and hold her hands down. But she got hold of that wood and hit me." He held out his hand to show the blood on it. "I'm the victim here!"

"Thank you." Carson turned. "Now, Ms. Freemont, do you want to share your side of story?"

Anne launched into the hunt for Faith and how they had found her in the kitchen. "I was only locking up the front door. I thought you were the person I saw in the yard this morning."

"What person?" a chorus of voices echoed. She looked up to see Kandi, Jeff, and a few others had returned and stood in the entry hall off the living room.

Stewart spoke first. "You saw someone on the property? Who was it?"

Anne sighed. "I didn't get a good look."

She glanced over to see Jeff's shoulders relaxing. He bent down and whispered something to Kandi, who nodded. Clearing his throat to get attention, he said, "Sheriff Carson, am I free to go? I've got work to do."

"Yes. You can go. If I have any questions, I know where to find you." He turned back to Stewart. "Mr. Rogers, what would you like to do?"

"I told you. I want you to arrest her!" He pointed at Anne.

"Arrest me? For what?" She rose out of her chair. "I was only defending myself!"

Stewart ticked off the words with his fingers. "Trespassing. Assault. Property damage."

The chief nodded at his deputy, who pulled his cuffs from his belt, and headed toward Anne. The deputy intoned, "You have the right…"

"You've got to be kidding me!" She backed toward the wall.

The deputy continued, "…to remain silent. Anything you say can and will be…"

"Are you serious? You're arresting me?" Anne hated hearing the plea in her voice.

"I didn't break in. The door was open."

"Do you have the right to be in this house?" Carson regarded her with a stare.

"Well, I…" Anne fought back tears.

The deputy's word's cut through the clutter of the moment "…used against you…" The words faded as she felt her arm being pulled back and the snap of cuffs on her wrists.

Stunned, Anne faced Stewart, and a burst of anger hit her. "Oh, so this is how it is. I hope you're happy now. You probably killed your uncle, and now you're trying to divert suspicion."

Stewart jumped to his feet. "Why, you little—" He fell back into the chair, grasping his head with both hands.

Anne stuck out her tongue at him. It was juvenile, but she felt better. Until she saw the sheriff's gaze on her.

Luckily, she wouldn't have to bear more of his wrath as medics had arrived and set to work on Stewart's wound.

She debated whether she was sorry he was hurt or if she felt he had gotten his just desserts for attacking her.

With the sheriff holding her upper arm, the two headed toward the front door. She moaned when she spied the media van parked on the street. When the reporter caught sight of Anne, she seized the photojournalist, who started capturing Anne's shame for the entire world.

Anne tried to turn away but was restrained by the deputy from behind. She gazed imploringly up at the sheriff.

Carson took her coat and placed it over her head. "Keep watching my boots," he murmured.

She nodded and choked back a sob. Ignoring the barrage of questions, she put one foot in front of the other until they reached the patrol car. At the vehicle door, she felt a pressure on her head as she was lowered into the back seat.

Tears dripped from her eyes down her cheeks. *This was supposed to be a new start. A great place. Instead, I find a dead body, tick off the only real friend I have in this town, and now I'm going to jail for assault.*

As soon as they were away from the cameras and the neighborhood, the car's tires crunched on gravel as it came to a stop. Her door was opened and the coat was removed. Pulling a handkerchief from his back pocket, the chief wiped her eyes, and then her nose. He then shut the door and moved back around to the driver's seat. He got on the radio. "Thelma, is there a white van out front of the station?"

The woman came back with an affirmative.

Oh, great. I get to walk the gauntlet twice.

Their eyes met in the rearview mirror. "Don't worry. We have a back way where we take prisoners into the jail area."

She muttered under her breath, "Wonderful."

"I could always take you in the front if you prefer." She noticed the crinkles at the edges of his eyes.

He must be getting a kick out of this. She wished she could say something, but she knew when she'd been beaten. "No, no. That's fine. Thank you."

When they arrived at the station, he ushered her into a dull room of metal desks and khaki-colored walls. Two cells sat over to the side. She shivered at the sight of them, recalling her visit with Kandi. The cuffs were removed and she rubbed her arms to get the circulation flowing.

"Take a seat." He motioned to her while he hung up his hat and coat.

She slumped into the chair, the hard, cold metal frame chilling her back.

Carson pulled out a bunch of forms and set them on his desk.

A woman, around eighty, entered the room. She wore a loud polyester top and slacks with a crease sewn down the front. Her white-gray permed hair formed a halo of tight curls around her face. She wore bright red lipstick that crept past her upper lip and melded into a light mustache.

Anne instinctively felt this was a woman you didn't mess with.

"Carson, I told that woman she had to move the van or be ticketed for loitering. They're gone."

"Thanks, Thelma." He scooted his chair closer to the desk.

The woman smiled at him, then turned to Anne. Her face took on a scowl, and she looked down her nose at Anne.

Anne instinctively tightened her arms.

Carson glanced up. "You can go now." She retreated, leaving a floral reminder of White Shoulders perfume.

He sighed. "I could use something to drink. How 'bout you?" She nodded and rubbed her hands up and down her arms again. He went to a refrigerator in a little kitchen area off the back. "Not much in here. Some juice, a few sodas, water."

"Just some water, please." He grabbed a paper cup and poured some water from a canister he'd pulled from the fridge. He handed the water to her, then popped open a can of grapefruit juice, which he guzzled.

"Are you going to book me? Am I going to get fingerprinted or ...or ..."—she gulped—"...searched?"

"We're a small operation. I've worked this town for more than twenty years. We'll give it fifteen more minutes."

Curious, she said, "Fifteen more minutes?"

"Yep."

Fifteen minutes for what?

He leaned his chair back until he was balancing on two legs. They sat and stared at one another. Her gaze took in the room. The seconds on the wall clock ticked loudly in the silence.

"Is it okay if I get up?"

"Nope."

"Okay, then." She folded her hands in her lap and started picking at her nails.

Minutes ticked by. He stared. She fidgeted.

When the phone rang, it clamored so loudly that it caught Anne by surprise. The sheriff's chair fell back on all four legs. "Sheriff Carson speaking. ...Uh, huh. Yes... Yes...No...

Certainly...Will do. Thanks for calling." He set the phone receiver back in the cradle.

"Okay, you're free to go." He motioned.

"I ...I can go? Just like that?"

"Yep." He put the papers back in the drawer.

"Why?" She jumped up, happy to be free of the cold metal. A burden lifted.

"Stewart dropped the charges. He realizes now that you weren't breaking in and were just trying to protect yourself."

"I was. I wouldn't have hit him if I hadn't thought he was trying to kill me."

He retrieved a file and set it on his desk.

He looked up at her. "Here's the thing. I don't like paperwork. You're making a whole heck of a lot of paperwork for me. Don't do it again."

"I don't intend to." Anne waited for the all clear.

"Good." He stood. "Need me to call someone?"

Maybe he was okay after all. "No thanks. I think I'll go check on Hope and Faith while I'm in town."

He nodded and sat back down at his desk.

Just as she reached the door, he called out, "Hey, Nancy. Stay out of attics."

Oh, how she wished she could wipe that smirk off his face. She bit back her reply and made sure she slammed the door behind her.

Chapter Eighteen

Back at home, Anne made a hot cup of tea. It had been a crazy day and she needed to find some calm and some clarity. Taking her tea into the living room, she kindled a fire in the fireplace. Once the room was nice and toasty, Anne pulled up the armchair so she could rest her feet on the hearth. She thought back to Sorcha's mention of the threads. There were a lot of threads but no discernible pattern, at least that she could see. Now with the fire dying, Anne rose and headed to the dining room where she assembled the items she'd picked up at the local craft store. She got ready to set up her mind map. She attached paper from a drawing pad to the wall with shipping tape. With the wall covered in paper, she grabbed the other items she'd purchased—a set of markers, push pens, some red yarn, and some yellow yarn.

Okay. Where to begin? The actual murder.

Anne drew a circle in the middle of the white paper with Ralph's name in the center. Off to the left, she drew another circle. Inside it, she wrote Kandi. She connected the lines with another marker and wrote on top of the line "Neighbors." Underneath she wrote the word "Motive" and a question mark. Then she created a list.

Number one. Threat of chickens being killed.

Number two. Wanting to expand her property by buying Ralph out.

Number three.

Hmmmm. Nothing. Anne drew a series of question marks.

Mouser appeared in the doorway. She picked up the kitten. "You know what, Mouser? Finding the killer sure seems easier in books or movies." She stroked the kitten, who responded with a growing purr.

Anne sighed. No other motive came to mind for Kandi. Okay, dead end. Next. She set the kitten down on the floor. He stretched and then grabbed at an errant strand from a ball of yarn.

Anne drew smaller circles close to Ralph's circle. One circle for Stewart with a notation of nephew in parenthesis. Another circle for Faith (lost love). And one for Hope (daughter). She listed the various motives Stewart or Hope had to kill Ralph. Anne stepped back from the wall.

Wait a minute.

If Hope was Ralph's daughter, then she would be his rightful heir, not Stewart. Stewart said he got part of the property but it was probably a much smaller portion than Hope's. That would mean that Stewart really had a smaller motive to kill Ralph, whereas it increased Hope's motive due to Faith's declining health. Anne went back to the table and opened another packet of Sharpie markers. She pulled the red one out. She wrote an M for motive by each person's name. So far, Kandi had two, Stewart one and Hope three. She listed Hope's motives.

One. Held bitterness of growing up without her father.

Two. Ralph not helping with her mother.

Three. Possible inheritance and money.

But what about proof? Anne picked up a green marker. Unfortunately, the proof or evidence all pointed toward Kandi. She'd argued with Ralph. She had been seen with her hands on the axe, and her fingerprints were the only ones other than Ralph's.

But that left Anne with more questions. Why would Kandi move the murder weapon and hide it in her own yard? She could have simply wiped the handle clean, or if premeditated, she would have worn gloves. Plus, even if she had wanted Ralph's place, there could be no guarantee that she would win the bid for it.

Dead end.

How about the others? Anne thought back to the first time the group had met in the kitchen. They all had pretty much the same alibi—none really—sleeping. She stared at the wall. Using the push pins and yarn, she made connection paths. Still, nothing jumped out.

Okay, next level. She added Eliza to the list. What could possibly be her motive? Anne couldn't come up with a single thing. Oh, wait. He *had* hit her car, broken the taillight, and banged up her bumper. She was pretty picky about her things. Opportunity? Yes, just like all the others. But if people killed others because they'd damaged their vehicle, there'd be a whole lot of dead people around.

Think, Anne.

She recalled their initial meeting and Eliza saying how Kandi had helped her so much when she first arrived. But just because someone is nice to you doesn't mean you go kill someone for them. Another dead end.

Who next? Oh yes, her favorite suspect. Jeff. Anne knew she'd have to be careful not to let her prejudice against Jeff cloud her judgment. She added a circle and attached it to Kandi.

Motive? He had plenty. If she knew his type—*and she did*—he wanted to get his hands on Kandi's money. What better way than to get her out of the picture? So Jeff and Hope seemed to have the motive that often trumped many others—money.

Anne ran her hands through her hair. She remembered the meeting in Kandi's kitchen. She grabbed her phone and opened up the camera. The photo was small, but she was still able to read the list of names that the group had added at the prior meeting. She felt she could cross off the first name she spied on their list, but for fun she added her own name to the board. She chuckled as she listed her so-called motives.

One. Hates men.

Two. Mad because of her falling into his compost pile.

Three. Wanted his property because hers is turning into a money pit.

"What do you say, Mouser? Do you think I did it?" The kitten stopped its play and stared at her. "I know, I know. I had opportunity. Right next door. My alibi of sleeping sucks."

Mouser turned and ran through the door.

Anne shivered. Ugh, Mouser probably heard or saw a

mouse. She yelled, "I forgive you, Mouser. I know you don't think I did it." Geez. Now she was talking to a cat.

She reviewed the other names on the list. Two she didn't know at all. Even those at the meeting had argued about them being suspects. That stopped her. What about people you'd never think of? Like the postman? Someone coming up from the trail? Or a serial killer drifter? A time traveling telegrapher? Or the person you'd least expect—like Sam.

Anne drew his name in a circle. What could be Sam's motive? She couldn't think of anything. However, he said he often jogged along the path, and she'd seen that he had a balaclava in his pocket. Was there something about Sam she was missing?

Anne looked back at the wall.

Could Faith in a lucid moment have killed Ralph? Of everyone listed on the wall, she had been treated the worst by Ralph. He had left her pregnant and alone. She'd raised a daughter by herself. Even though she'd refused his proposal after his wife and son were killed, he hadn't provided for her or Hope. Though Sorcha said he'd tried and Faith had refused his money. Maybe Faith just told people that. Maybe she'd asked him for money, and he'd refused?

No. Not after hearing Ralph's story from Sorcha. More likely, her pride got in the way. Did she even realize how hard it was on Hope to care for her while trying to run a full-time business?

She added Faith's name to the wall between Ralph and Hope. Could she have had the strength to kill Ralph?

Really, when it came down to it, all you needed was momentum and gravity would do the rest.

Anne sat down at the table and rested her head in her hands.

A mewing caught her attention. The cat had returned. She picked him up and stroked his fur. "Mouser, I don't know if I am going to be able to help Kandi. I just don't see any pattern. All I see are threads." She sighed.

"Time for a break." She carried Mouser into the kitchen where she rewarded him with a saucer of milk. She pulled on boots and grabbed her jacket from the hook. Opening the back door Anne breathed in deeply as the crisp fresh air and scent of the forest refreshed her.

Yet apprehension began to take hold as she walked toward Ralph's. Would Stewart accuse her of trespassing again? Or would Carson still be skulking about? He would most likely be gone now, but nonetheless, she peeked around the lilacs to make sure no one was there before proceeding into the yard.

Off to her right was the compost area. Further to her left was a pile of wood. Some split, others waiting. She walked toward the area and noticed that it was very close to a bend in the woods. She could make out the marks where Stewart had come up on his skis and tossed them to the side. A short path led into the forest so she followed it. Her feet sunk into the accumulated snow still dense from the shade.

Anne turned back and was met with a clear view from the main path up to the wood pile. She stopped and took it all in. When the chill began to seep into her extremities, she headed back up the hill. She glanced down at the wood pile. Yes, more wood had definitely been cut since the first time she'd seen Kandi and Ralph. But when had Ralph done the cutting?

The more she dug, the fewer answers she found, and the more questions emerged. Frustrated at getting nowhere with her snooping, she decided to call it a day on the detective work.

Her phone vibrated in her pocket.

Chapter Nineteen

Anne answered her phone. It was Eliza calling to see if Anne could drive her home from the hospital.

Eliza was sitting on the side of her bed when Anne arrived and as usual she was impeccably dressed. No one would know she'd been in an accident except for the bandage adorning the left side of her face. "Thank you for coming." She spoke as if she were accepting guests at a formal party.

Anne snatched up Eliza's Louis Vuitton overnight bag as the nurse helped Eliza into the wheelchair. As they moved toward the door, another nurse headed toward them carrying a banker's box. "Here. Don't forget this. It's yours too." Eliza held the box on her lap as they proceeded out the door.

Taking the box from Eliza, Anne stowed it in the back. She climbed into the truck while the nurse helped Eliza. Anne pulled on her seatbelt. "Are they going to be able to repair your car?"

"Unfortunately, no. I am afraid that I must find another vehicle." Eliza placed her head against the back window. The strain of the accident was painfully evident on her face.

"Sure you're all right?"

"Thanks for the concern. I'm actually feeling much better. I'd been struggling with sleeping well and hadn't been able to do my daily runs."

"You run?"

"Yes. The trail circles around the lake as well as around the town. I try to complete a daily ten-mile circuit. However, lately I'd been lucky to get in three to five. I've been too tired to do more." She shifted and faced Anne. "Do you run? We could run together some time."

"No. I don't run. And if you see me running you better run too because something bad would be chasing me."

Eliza smiled. "I'll remember that." Her smile faded and dread passed over her face.

Anne grimaced. "Did I say something wrong? Are you okay?"

"No. It is not your fault. Some things are best left in the dark where they belong." She turned to look out of the passenger window, thus cutting off any further conversation.

What was Eliza afraid of? Was she hiding something that threatened her strong outward composure?

Anne had forgotten that Eliza lived out close to Sam. They passed the cut-off to his house and drove for another half mile until Eliza signaled to slow down. The unmarked road was partly hidden by a stand of trees and if you didn't know about the road off the highway, you would drive by without ever seeing it.

She pulled into the gap in the trees. "Wow. Don't you want to put up a marker here?"

"No. I prefer it this way."

Anne glanced at the woman. With her busy schedule, maybe Eliza preferred seclusion.

Eliza's road had been graded and was a much easier drive than Sam's. Eliza motioned ahead. "Here we are." Anne stopped the truck. The road continued on into the forest. When Anne looked quizzically at what appeared to be a grassy hill, Eliza broke out in a big smile. "What? Don't you see it?"

"See what?" Anne squinted.

Eliza pointed past Anne. All Anne could see was an open patch of hilly ground against the trees. Then, as she continued to focus her gaze, she realized the hill seemed out of place with the rest of the surrounding grounds. Pipes were visible.

Anne opened her door. "Wow. Is it one of those earth houses?"

Eliza replied yes. She opened the door. With Anne's help, she tentatively placed her feet on the ground. As Eliza held onto the door, Anne grabbed the luggage and then came alongside her. "Here, take my arm."

"Thank you." Eliza clutched tightly to Anne's arm and the pair gingerly made their way on a flagstone path Anne hadn't noticed before. As they slowly made their way down the shady path, the entrance to the house appeared. This dwelling and Sam's rustic cabin were as different as night and day. The structure's eastern wall was a bank of windows with rock wall supports, a cross of modern and Colorado rustic.

Eliza unlocked the door and led Anne into the home. The expansive windows in the living area faced the lake. She helped Eliza into a spacious bedroom with more views to the lake and north along the forest. A deck opened off the bedroom and Anne spied a winding path up into the trees. This must be the trail everyone talked about.

"This is amazing. It's a bit like sleeping in the forest."

Eliza smiled and pointed. "The original cabin is not far away when you take the path. I plan to redo it this coming year as a guest house and art studio."

"I didn't know you were an artist."

"Yes. I love working with various mediums. I made all the pottery throughout the house." Leaving the luggage, they returned to the living area.

Anne took in the view. "This house is so open and airy. It's delightful. I can certainly see why you built here. The views are gorgeous."

"I enjoy it. You should come spend the weekend with me some time. You may not enjoy running, but we could walk around the lake."

"Speaking of that, does this trail go into the city and past my house?"

"Yes. It does. I used to run that way quite a bit." Eliza shivered.

"You don't anymore?"

Eliza hesitated. "I decided to try another route. It's away from town." She studied her hands. "But then I had the wreck."

"What happened that night?"

"Please—sit." The women took chairs facing the lake

before Eliza began. "Honestly, I don't remember. I'd returned from an overseas trip, so jet-lag had set in. The next thing I knew I woke up in the hospital."

"That's scary."

"I guess I decided to go into town for something. But the knock on my head makes it so fuzzy. I can't remember what really happened." She swayed and clutched the chair arm.

"Are you sure you're okay? Do I need to call the doctor?"

"No. I'm fine. I think it's just standing up and moving around so much after being in bed for so long. Listen, I know this is a big imposition, but would you consider staying here this evening? I don't want anything else…"

"Certainly. Let me go back to my place and grab an overnight bag. I can also pick us up something for dinner. What do you want?"

"That is very thoughtful. Something light would be nice. You select what you would like." Tears welled up in her eyes. Eliza sighed and closed her eyes. "I'm so tired. I can't do it anymore."

Anne reached over and took Eliza's hand. "Listen, you've had a bad accident. I'm sure you can rework upcoming plans and take some time off." Anne smiled at her. "I've found that no matter how bad things seem, they always tend to work out."

"Yes. You are correct. It will work itself out."

Outside, Anne remembered the box in the back of her truck. As she pulled the box toward her, it caught the lip of the truck bed and the contents tumbled onto the drive. Eliza's purse fell open and a prescription bottle rolled out. A sleep aid. A journal had also fallen open. As Anne reached to pick it up, an old photograph fell out of the pages.

In the picture, a younger Eliza stood next to a group of girls. They were all smiling, the very picture of youth. Anne didn't recognize the background. It had the look of a dry grass prairie with a dusty clay brick building blocking most of the landscape.

A photo from when Eliza was younger? Yet she's still beautiful, if not even more gorgeous now. So why does she only do modeling that doesn't show her face? Anne returned the picture and began to retrieve the other items.

Finally, she picked up a book that had fallen from the box. Anne read the title—*Reasonable Doubt*. The tome centered on court cases where juries had failed to convict due to reasonable doubt.

Looks like she's trying to help Kandi. I'll have to talk to her about it later.

Anne hauled the box over to the walkway. She'd take it in when she returned. Back at her house, she quickly pulled together an overnight bag. She stuffed the duffle bag with a nightgown and a fresh outfit for the morning. She'd called into the town café and had them make up a spring salad and bowls of tomato basil soup. Finally, she picked up a bouquet of gladiolas. Bird of paradise suited Eliza more, but the town florist carried basic flowers that would sell best.

When Anne arrived back at Eliza's, the box was no longer on the pathway. She went up to the door and knocked. She heard the door unlock and Eliza appeared in a caftan the color of sunset. "Wow. You look beautiful. That's a stunning dress. You're really blessed with your looks."

"Some might say cursed."

"Well, it wouldn't be me." She followed Eliza and sat the bags on the counter.

"Thank you for the food and the flowers. You're very sweet." She retrieved a set of vases in varying sizes.

As Anne sliced a baguette from the café, Eliza arranged the flowers. As she worked, Anne scanned the area. No box. Eliza must have put it in her bedroom.

Anne placed the bread on a plate. "I see you found the box outside."

Eliza gazed at Anne. "Yes. I went outside to check for any packages that may have been delivered while I was in hospital." She replied softly, "I will return shortly." When she came back, she held up another caftan in the color of a deep minty green. "I will not be offended if you would prefer to continue to wear your current outfit. However, this is much more comfortable."

"I'd love to wear that. Thank you." Anne moved toward the stairs to the lower room.

"No. Please." Eliza motioned toward her room. "I have put on new sheets. I wish for you to sleep here."

"I couldn't possibly impose and take you away from your own bed," Anne asserted.

"I've been sleeping downstairs for a while. To break habits....I mean, they say you should always spend a night or two in your guest room so you know if anything is missing." She didn't elaborate further on why she'd vacated her wonderful master bedroom.

"But please, you are my guest and I insist."

She ushered Anne to the room and then closed the door. Anne stepped into the lush dressing room and pulled off her boots, jeans, and top. She remembered Eliza being barefoot, so she shucked her socks too. Dropping the caftan over her body felt like being enclosed in a warm silky wrap. "Oh my."

She ran her hands up and down the sleeves. Turning, she looked at herself in the full-length mirror. Whereas the caftan hit Eliza mid-calf, Anne's shorter stature provided a floor-length gown. Darts provided some shape and while the dress was loose on Eliza, the flowing gown fit Anne nicely. Anne laid her dirty clothing on top of her duffel bag.

Anne exited to find lit candles all around the room. The table had been set with beautiful pottery, and Eliza had set the food on the table.

"Here, I'm supposed to be helping you, and you're doing all the work," Anne exclaimed.

"Please do not think that. I appreciate your being here. You look lovely in your dress."

"This is probably the most wonderful thing I've had on in my life, and I've had some nice clothing in the past. It doesn't compare to how this feels." She walked to the table. "The temperature in this house is so lovely. I would have thought it would be cold with all the windows, but I love these heated floors." The warmth on her feet radiated up into her legs.

"The house has geothermal heating. The floors are heated as you said. I prefer to go barefoot when I can and this allows that no matter how much snow is outside."

Anne wiggled her toes. "It's certainly very nice."

As they ate, Eliza shared about the celebrities she'd met and times she had been their hands or served as a body double. On questioning from Eliza, Anne shared much of the backstory around her miscarriage and divorce from Duke.

Eliza set down her spoon. "I'm so sorry to hear what you went through. The world can be so cruel."

"Do you have any brothers or sisters?" Anne took a bite of salad.

"I had a sister." Eliza sighed deeply and gazed down into her lap.

Had. "I'm sorry. I didn't mean to pry."

"It is fine. But I do not wish to talk about it now."

"Okay." Anne wiped her hands and gathered the dress folds around her legs.

Eliza stifled a yawn. "I'm very tired. I believe I will retire for the evening." She stood and picked up the plates.

"Let me take care of the dishes. You go and get some sleep." Anne rose.

"That is most kind." She moved away from the table.

"Did the doctor give you something for sleep?"

"I no longer take sleep aids. They have bad side effects." Eliza went downstairs.

"Okay. Well, good night then," Anne called after her.

She cleaned up the plates and pondered why Eliza had said she didn't take sleeping pills anymore. She'd definitely seen the bottle with Eliza's name on it. Why didn't Eliza want to admit she took a sleep aid?

Anne blew out the candles and watched as the moon's

reflection played off the mirror of the lake. Once in bed, she tossed and turned over the night's conversation. While much of it had been light conversation, they'd discussed Kandi's predicament as well.

When Anne brought up the fact of the axe being found in Kandi's yard, Eliza replied strangely, "That is what I do not understand. Who moved that axe? And why did they move it?"

Anne fell asleep to myriad thoughts. A sound brought her instantly awake. The bedroom door handle turned. Her breath caught in her throat.

A figure entered.

Eliza.

The light of the moon helped Anne see Eliza's silhouette as she moved silently over to the dressing room and closed the door. No light appeared under the crack of the door.

Why doesn't she just turn on the light? Maybe she forgot something and doesn't want to wake me.

When Eliza returned, she was wearing a pair of leggings and a tank top. She also wore running shoes. Now sitting up in bed, Anne realized that Eliza hadn't once acknowledged her presence.

She's sleepwalking!

Anne wanted to speak but fear kept her tongue in check. Hadn't she heard not to wake up sleepwalkers?

Eliza moved toward a dresser. She opened the drawer, pulled out a pair of gloves, and placed them on her hands. She also added a balaclava to hold back her hair.

Finally, she moved to the door and went out on to the deck off the bedroom. From there, she set off on a jog.

Instead of circling away from the city, she headed toward town.

Anne grabbed the clothes she'd discarded earlier. Eliza shouldn't be running after her accident.

However, by the time Anne had gotten dressed, Eliza was nowhere to be seen. No way could Anne catch up with her. Plus she could barely see in the darkness. How was Eliza able to run so effortlessly without light?

Unsure of what to do next, Anne sat down on a rock. Should she call the police? And say what? That a woman was running on a trail in the forest?

Finally, she heard a twig snap. She rose to see Eliza headed her way. Yet once again, Eliza ignored Anne's presence and swept by her at a quick pace. Anne scrambled after the woman. Inside, Eliza went to her dressing room. When she emerged, she'd changed out of her running gear and back into her pajamas. Eliza then slid into her own bed and turned over on her side.

Anne leaned over quietly and gazed at the woman. Eliza was sound asleep.

Anne sighed. Oh well, I wanted to see that sunrise over the lake. Now I'll get my chance.

She grabbed a blanket from the end of the bed and headed out to the deck. She cuddled down into the lounger and quickly fell fast asleep again.

Soft light hit her eyelids.

Anne blinked as her eyes spied the morning's first soft glow painting the lake and surroundings with a stroke of pink. As the light brightened in the sky, a flock of geese flew past. Anne sat up and hugged her knees to her chest.

The glass patio door opened behind her.

Eliza came outside and sat down across from Anne. The woman stared at her and then broke down in sobs.

"I killed him. I killed Ralph."

Chapter Twenty

Anne advised Eliza to call a lawyer before contacting the police. Eliza concurred and contacted one based in Denver. As they waited for the attorney to arrive, the two women faced each other.

Anne sat in stunned silence. Even though Eliza had confessed to killing Ralph, Anne simply couldn't believe this woman had done such a horrible deed. Why would Eliza have killed Ralph?

Neither spoke. A clock ticked loudly from across the room. A bird landed on the deck outside.

Anne glanced over at Eliza. The woman had paled and sweat clung to her face and chest. Their eyes met. Eliza broke down in deep gut-wrenching sobs. Finally, when the tsunami of emotion had passed, Anne handed Eliza a box of tissues. Eliza wiped her face and took in a deep halting breath.

She searched Anne's face, then spoke. "I'm originally from Ethiopia. We were poor. Very poor. My parents found out about an agency looking for workers." She wrung her hands.

"Some men came to our village. Searching for models.

My sister and I were thrilled. They pointed at me. They told my parents my sister could work in a hotel. We would be leaving our parents, our homes, and our life as we knew it. I would not leave. Not unless my sister could come with me."

Eliza stopped, and buried her head in her hands. When she looked up again, tears blotted her cheeks again. "If I could take it back, I would do anything to change our fate. We were to go with them the following day. They selected some other girls for both jobs." Eliza rose and went to a closet where she pulled the photograph Anne had seen earlier out of the notebook. "This is us. All smiles." She trembled. "If we had only known the hell we were going to."

She pointed to a young woman in the picture. "This is my sister. Adanech. My real name is K…Konjit." Eliza stumbled over her name like someone struggling to speak a new language.

Anne didn't know how to respond. She waited for the woman to continue.

Eliza braced her shoulders, her back ramrod straight. "We left our home. After a short while, our car stopped. We were told to get into a van. I still remember vividly how hot and cramped it was." Her jaw clenched. "So many girls."

"Please, let me make some tea for us." With Eliza's instruction, Anne prepared green tea. She brought the cups over to where Eliza sat and handed her the cup. After they had sipped in silence for a time, Eliza continued her story.

"We drove for so long. When they finally opened the

doors, I had no idea where we were. They rushed us out of the van. We were in a compound. That was the first time my confusion turned to fear. Men with military-style weapons stood guard. One yelled at us to get inside. Girls started screaming. Running. One was beaten in front of us. When she became unconscious, they dragged her inside."

"Eliza, if this is too painful..." Anne spoke softly.

"No, I've been carrying this burden alone for too long. Will you allow me to continue?" Eliza waited.

"Please." Anne wasn't sure how this tied to Ralph's murder, but it might be best to let Eliza speak now.

"My sister and I were put into a room together. Two to a room. No windows. Someone brought food and water... and a bucket. We waited. After a while we heard a door open to another room. Even through the concrete walls, we heard the screams. Then it would be quiet again. Another cell opening and closing. Screams."

She closed her eyes and breathed deeply. "Then our door opened."

"Two guards entered. Another man was with them. A white man. He looked at my sister and then me. Guards forced me to stand. He instructed me to turn around. I was so afraid. I didn't move. The white man turned and slapped Adanech. Hard. I rushed toward her. A guard grabbed me. My sister pulled herself up from the ground. He hit her again—hard across the face. Her mouth ...so bloody. This time she didn't get up as he punched her again. I pleaded. Begged him to stop. I said I would do what he asked. I know now that this is what he wanted. Otherwise, he would have continued the beating.

"He told me to turn around. Remove my clothing. I hesitated. He kicked my sister. I took off my clothes and stood there in my humiliation. He asked if I was a virgin. I nodded, yes. Then he asked my sister." Eliza stopped and wiped her eyes, the pain etched on her face.

"Why she said no, I'll never understand. I can only guess that she thought it would protect me. He told the guards not to touch me. They raped my sister in front of my eyes. When they found out she *had* been a virgin, they beat her some more."

"Oh, Eliza. I don't know what to say." She moved over next to the woman and took her hands in her own.

"They left us alone for about a week. We didn't know if it was night or day. Then the white man returned. He told me that I was going to meet a very important man. If I tried to run, my sister would be killed."

"Were you worried they would kill her anyway?"

"No. She was still of use to them." She stared at Anne. "She was fourteen."

"Oh my god." Anne clutched at her throat. "How old were you?"

Eliza spoke softly. "Thirteen. However, one man had specifically asked for an Ethiopian virgin. I was taken to his yacht." She sighed and took a sip of her tea. "The man asked to speak to the white man, but my guards said that he didn't attend transactions. The man—they called him Mr. Smith—nodded. One of his men came forward with a briefcase filled with American dollars. After the men left, Mr. Smith told the guards to take me below."

Anne's stomach tightened, the fear of that past moment palpable between them.

Eliza cupped her hands in her lap. "I was terrified. I shook so terribly that they ended up supporting me. I waited for over an hour. Finally, he came. I dropped to my knees and begged him to not hurt me."

Eliza took a sip of the lukewarm tea. She glanced out at the lake. Anne prepared for the worst.

Eliza continued, "Mr. Smith lifted me up from the ground and put his fingers to his lips. Then, very loudly, he said, "Take a bath—I don't want to touch filth." I was confused, but followed him into the bathroom. He started the tub and the shower. Then turned on horrific hard-rock music.

"It was deafening. Smith opened a cabinet. Inside was a safe. There was another hidden safe inside the safe. He was with an international secret service organization. They were trying to take down human trafficking cartels. They had hoped to capture the white man, but he continued to evade them. They needed someone on the inside. By the end of the evening I'd been fitted with a tracking chip. I told him about my sister and he said they would do everything in their power to save her too."

Anne could barely believe the horror Eliza had endured. Anne had heard of human trafficking but had never personally met a survivor. She waited as Eliza took another sip of tea.

Eliza composed herself before resuming the story. "I returned to the compound with the story that the man had to go away on business and wasn't able to finish the transaction. He would return for me. This ensured I would not be raped. They allowed me to rejoin Adanech. She wasn't eating and had developed a fever. I implored them for a doctor, but they just laughed. Then one day a few weeks after I'd returned, I heard men shouting. Gunfire. My sister and I tried to escape out an unlocked door, but one of the guards saw us. He fired his gun. My sister pushed me out the door. She was shot. She died in my arms."

Anne gasped. "Eliza, I'm so sorry. I don't know what to say. I'm so sorry for your loss."

"Thank you." Eliza wiped more tears from her eyes. "That was many years ago. The agency helped me to come to America because I had become a target since I'd exposed the operation. I was placed in protection for many more years. I finally decided if I had to live that way for the rest of my life, they had killed me as much as they had taken the life of my sister and taken me from my family forever. I started working as a model's assistant. Later, I stepped in for models' hands and feet, and as a body double. My career took off."

So that explained why Eliza never showed her face in pictures. "I'm sure this is going to come across as very rude, but I don't know how else to say it. Why did you come to Carolan Springs? If you're still trying to stay away from these people, wouldn't a town with a more diverse ethnicity work better?"

Eliza threw back her head and laughed loudly. "Yes. I would have thought so too. But I have the best protection I can receive by staying."

"What? Sorry, but that makes no sense."

"You have not lived in the town long enough. However, you will find that people here are very protective of its residents. The first few times I visited, I would ask how to get to Kandi's house, and the people would react with *Who?*

At first, yes, I thought that the town was racist. But that is not the case at all. They are, in fact, very caring to anyone and everyone. I guess they feel sharing about someone without their permission is disrespectful to that person. Though talking about them *in* the town is another thing." She laughed again, breaking the somber moment.

Anne considered what Eliza said. *I bet they hate the outside media I brought here recently.*

Eliza retrieved more tea. "So if anyone were to ask about a tall black woman, the people here would instantly know that I don't want to see anyone asking for me. And, even better, they would contact me immediately."

"How do you know? Are you sure?"

"Yes. I once had someone from a photo shoot in Denver say they wanted to come out to dinner. I recommended they come here. Finally, they called me and asked why the people were so unfriendly and unhelpful in giving directions."

"Eliza, I can't imagine what you've gone through. You've had horrific things happen to you. I, for one, can certainly understand about moving here to escape something. But what I can't understand is what this has to do with Ralph's murder."

Eliza moaned. "I still can't believe I killed him."

"Are you saying that you don't know if you killed him? I'm sorry, but I'm confused. And you just don't seem like the killer type. Now, Stanley's wife, I wouldn't put it past her. You know, sweet little old lady… "

Eliza burst out laughing. Anne joined in.

"Thank you, sweet Anne. I needed that." She stopped and smoothed down her robe. She glanced at a nearby clock. "We still have some time before the lawyer arrives from Denver. We need to get dressed, and then I could use some coffee and something to eat. You?"

"Sounds good."

After Eliza dressed, Anne retreated to the bathroom and dressed, her mind awhirl with so many thoughts, her emotions overwhelmed at all she'd seen and heard. She didn't know how to feel. One thing she knew for certain was that she felt safe with Eliza. Yet, her confession to Ralph's murder seemed off. Something was still missing.

Back in the kitchen, Anne watched the woman go through the motions of setting the coffee to brew. Almost mechanically, Eliza placed granola, yogurt, and fruit on the table. When they sat down to eat, Eliza spoke.

"I've been trying to figure out what happened. It's because of my sleep. When we were in captivity, they would constantly change the lighting. You would be sleeping and the lights would come on. You would be awake, and they would turn the lights off and you would have to sit in darkness. I later heard it's a standard form of torture to create mental exhaustion. You never knew what to expect. Ever since then, a sound sleep has been difficult. This is why I moved out here. I feel safe, and I can sleep easier as I can see in every direction. But last year, I began having nightmares again. I finally went to a doctor who prescribed me these." She moved to the kitchen trashcan and dug out a bottle of prescription medication.

"The first night I slept fine. But then, I would have these vivid dreams. Or I would wake up and find myself in my jogging clothes.

Tears sprang to her eyes. "Then Ralph was murdered. I liked Ralph. Why would I want to kill him? Yet, I remember pieces of my dream from that night. I was running along the path behind the houses. I heard something. Our cell door was open. I needed to flee before they returned. I had to save my sister. I sprinted out of the door. Of course, there was no door.

"Then I saw the white man. My sister headed toward him. I had to stop him. I ran. We struggled. I wouldn't let him hurt my sister. He shoved me to the ground. I blacked out—or fell asleep—or …" She threw her hands in the air. "I don't know!

"When I woke up, Ralph was lying on his back on the ground. I ran to my house. In the morning, I was in my pajamas in my bed. I thought at the time that it had all been a nightmare."

"Wait. So you were really running, but you thought you were running in a dream?"

"I think that's true, but I can't be sure."

"The door you saw. Is that the area from the path onto Ralph's property?" Anne didn't wait for Eliza's response before thinking aloud. "Now that I think of it, with the trees overhanging, that area does look somewhat like a door." She paused. "Eliza, why are you telling me all this? Shouldn't you wait for the lawyer?"

Eliza reached across the table and took Anne's hand. "Because I trust you, Anne. I know if anyone can help me make sense of this mess, it's you. That's why I felt I could release my burden. I consider you a good friend."

Anne squeezed Eliza's hand. "I consider you a good friend too." Anne felt certain that Eliza hadn't meant to kill Ralph. "Okay, Eliza, I've got some more questions. In your dream, you grabbed the axe and fought with Ralph. But if you were sleeping, it had to be nighttime. No one would be outside then. It doesn't make sense."

"I used to run every morning at five o'clock. Ralph was always up early too. I'd often see him in the café if I decided to go there for breakfast after my run."

"So he was in his yard—doing what?"

"I don't know. All I know is that I saw this white man heading toward my sister. I had to stop him."

"Your sister?" Anne motioned with her fork. "Did you see someone else?"

"I'm sorry. I don't know. Some of it is as clear as you sitting across from me. And some is fuzzy or I can't remember at all." Eliza poured more coffee for them both.

"So you grabbed the axe, and you struggled."

"Yes, I believe so."

"Then you either fell or were pushed?" Anne leaned toward Eliza.

"As far as I can remember, that's correct. I think we both fell."

"And you lost consciousness or whatever it was for a time. How long before you came to your senses again?"

Eliza concentrated. "I'm not sure. Probably not long. At that point, I don't know if I was awake or still in that dreamlike state. I saw him lying on the ground with his eyes closed. I got up and ran back to the path."

"So you didn't check to see if he was dead?"

Eliza shook her head. "I know that I should have but at the time I thought I was still dreaming."

"And the reason that your prints weren't on the axe was because you were wearing black gloves."

Eliza stiffened. "I suppose so. Yes."

"So you left. Ralph was sprawled on his back and you ran."

"I'm sorry, but I just can't remember."

Anne patted her hand.

"What about the car accident?"

"That's when I knew that I could be the one who killed Ralph. I was asleep when I got behind the wheel. I didn't remember getting in the car or driving. All I remember was waking up in the hospital. That's when I said I'd never take those pills again. Unfortunately, it sometimes has lingering side-effects, hence my run last night."

"But why didn't you say something?"

"I was afraid the cartel would find me. I needed time to think. But then they accused Kandi. I thought she'd be released, but then all the evidence pointed to her committing the murder."

The doorbell rang. They glanced over to see a man standing outside the entry. The lawyer had arrived.

Eliza stood to answer the door, but Anne pulled on her arm, "One last thing. Why did you move the axe?"

"I didn't move it."

Chapter Twenty-One

Anne hugged Eliza. "Be strong. We're going to keep working on this."

Eliza didn't respond, but nodded. The attorney had informed the police that he would escort Eliza to the station where she would turn herself in. Eliza got in the lawyer's Mercedes.

Anne followed the pair in her truck. After the Mercedes turned onto the main road, a cruiser pulled in behind the attorney's vehicle. Looked like the sheriff's office was ensuring Eliza's arrival.

Sheriff Carson. She saw his frown at seeing her as he drove past.

"Shoot. Bet I'll be getting a visit later today." Anne made no move to join the parade. Her hands tightly gripped the steering wheel. Poor Eliza. Her outward facade hid a broken reality of a life brutally torn apart. Anne felt certain Eliza had never intended to kill Ralph or hurt Kandi in the process. Now she needed their help. But something she'd said while recounting her story kept nibbling at Anne's mind.

Anne yanked her phone from her purse. She told

Kandi about Eliza's confession and she agreed to be at Anne's house by the time Anne arrived.

Kandi sat at the kitchen table. She jumped up when Anne entered. "I can't believe it! I can't see Eliza, *like*, hurting anyone."

"I agree. But she acknowledges she was at the scene when the murder occurred." The pair sat in the ladder-back chairs.

"Hmmm, I'm *like*, I mean, I'm happy that they won't think it's me anymore, and *like*, bummed it's Eliza." She twisted her mouth to the side, biting the inside of her cheek.

"Listen, I think we need to go back over that day. Or even maybe from the time I saw you with Ralph."

"Let me think." Her gaze rose to the left. She tilted her head right. "Let's see. So Rusty had gotten in Ralph's tomatoes—*again.*"

"Speaking of Rusty, I know you said she disappeared. Any news?"

"Craziest thing. All I can figure is she must have gotten out of the run. I know a bunch of foxes and other critters live in the forest. So I'm sure she's gone for good. I know it's silly, but I cried for days. Everyone thought it was about Ralph, and I know we were neighbors and all, but I barely knew him. He kept pretty much to himself." She shrugged her shoulders sheepishly.

"All right. Rabbit trail. So you went over to get her, and that's when you two got into a fight."

"Yep. He had Rusty in one hand and the axe in his other. I grabbed the axe handle to block him hurting Rusty."

"That's when I came around the lilacs," Anne interjected.

Kandi stuck her chin in the air. "Yep. That's right."

"So you were worried he was going to kill Rusty. Is that right?"

"Not really. I think he'd been chopping wood. If I get up early to see Jeff off for business trips, I can sometimes hear him."

"How early would you say?"

"Well, I guess it would be around four…or five in the morning. Those early flights are bad enough without the other nonsense you have to deal with at the airports."

Kandi twirled her hair with a finger. "So then I think, *like*, yes, you stepped too close to the compost pile and, *like*, fell into it." She snickered a bit. "It was kinda funny. Your arms doing a cartwheel." She stood and mimicked Anne's fall into the pile. Her face contorted in exaggerated horror.

"Yes. Ha. Ha. Real funny. Let's stay on track. Then what happened?"

Kandi sat back down. "Umm, let me think. I got Rusty, and Ralph kept the axe. I came over to help you up."

"What was Ralph doing then?"

"I think he put the axe down on the stump he used to split wood." Kandi crossed to the refrigerator and pulled out a container of juice. She retrieved two glasses and poured them each some before sitting back down.

"Then what happened?" Anne took a sip of the cold, tangy grapefruit juice.

"You were there for the rest. Ralph, *like*, told me to

keep my chicken out of his tomatoes, and I stuck out my tongue at him."

"When did Rusty disappear?"

"About that same time. I took Rusty home and put her in the run. I called Jeff and told him about what had happened with Ralph. He couldn't talk because he was in some kind of meeting with some, *like*, bigwigs."

"Okay, let's forget the chicken for now. Fast forward to when you found Ralph."

Kandi grimaced. "I couldn't find Rusty. I figured I better go see if she'd gone to Ralph's. I didn't want him getting mad again. I cut through over to his yard. He was lying face down on the compost pile. I turned him over and…that's when I saw the blood. Then I looked down and saw the blood all over my hands." She closed her eyes and took a deep breath. "I started screaming." She opened her eyes full of unshed tears. "That's when you came."

Anne reached over and hugged Kandi. "You're the best. Thank you!" She jumped up and performed a little victory dance. "I think I may have just solved the crime!" She squealed. "I can't believe it. I think I figured it out. Just like a real detective." She plopped back in her seat. "We have to have a meeting so I can present my hypothesis."

"Your what?" Kandi stared at Anne like she'd sprouted horns.

"My hypothesis." She saw Kandi's puzzled expression. "What I think happened to Ralph."

"Oh, okay. Where should we meet?"

"Where else does everyone meet when the crime is going to be solved—in the library!"

Sorcha had agreed to let them to use the library's alcove. Anne set to work attaching the information she'd collected from her dining room wall. She'd also gone to Sheriff Carson and asked if he'd be willing to allow her to present her ideas before he took Eliza off to Denver. Reluctantly, he'd agreed to attend and listen, even though Anne guessed it was more to see her make a fool out of herself. However, he wouldn't allow Eliza to be present at the meeting. When Anne told Eliza she'd be allowed to connect to the meeting online, Eliza informed her reluctant lawyer that she would attend.

Sorcha had lit a fire in the room and provided herbal tea, coffee, and cookies. The cozy atmosphere made it difficult to envision a discussion of murder. Anne glanced nervously at the group as people entered and took their seats. Kandi walked in with Jeff whose demeanor announced he didn't want to be there. Kandi found a seat next to Hope, who set down a bag close to a chair she'd pulled up for her mother. Sam sat in a chair next to the fireplace munching on one of Sorcha's chocolate cookies. Missy had begged to stay but had been shooed off by Sorcha. Stewart made his way in, quickly glanced around, and stood with his shoulder resting against the wall. He sat down when a chair was procured from the other room. Finally, in strode Carson and a deputy.

As the sheriff passed Sorcha, the woman touched her hair, lowered her eyes, and provided him with a sultry sounding hello.

Carson and Sorcha? Who would have guessed? No time to consider local romances now. Stay focused.

While everyone settled, Sam set up the computer's online meeting software. After ensuring Eliza and her attorney could hear and see the room, Anne spoke. "First, thank you all for coming. It's of utmost importance since Eliza will be entering her not-guilty plea in the next few weeks." Murmurs went around the room at her last statement. "I'd also like to say thank you to Sheriff Carson who allowed me to present my thoughts to you."

Everyone turned to look at Carson. He said, "Go ahead. I'm all ears."

Anne set out to present her case calmly and clearly. "As you may have heard, Eliza confessed to murdering Ralph."

Eliza's lawyer objected, but she silenced him.

Anne smiled. No way could she deal with a seasoned lawyer constantly interrupting her. "As you also know, I'm new to this town. Kandi's the first person I met, and she was a lifesaver when I injured myself right after arriving. I've gotten to know most of you in the last few months. However, I'm still an outsider. And being an outsider sometimes allows you to hear or see things others may miss. So that's why I've called you here today. I want to prove that I have good reason to believe, unequivocally, that Eliza did not kill Ralph. And neither did Kandi."

Eliza's lawyer relaxed back into his chair. Carson continued to gaze at Anne with a doubtful expression on his face.

Anne straightened. "When Kandi was arrested for Ralph's murder, we all came together to consider anyone who could have caused his death. I took the information you all had provided. As you can see, I've recreated it on this wall. What you see are the names of almost everyone here. I removed other names mentioned before after confirming their alibis through local sources. So what we have left are the following people: Kandi, Jeff—"

"I wasn't even in town when it happened," Jeff interrupted.

"Please. I will get to everyone in turn."

"Stewart…"

Stewart harrumphed and crossed his arms over his chest. Under his breath he said, "Waste of time."

"Hope, Faith, and of course, Eliza."

"What about *you*?" The sheriff interjected.

Anne sighed. Why was he trying to rile her? "I was sleeping. I'd dropped into bed after painting the front rooms. I also sleep with a white noise machine. This accounts for why I didn't hear anything. Also, I have absolutely *no* motive. None. Nada. Of course, you can certainly keep me as a suspect. Now, please, may I continue?"

Carson pursed his lips to hide his smirk. He nodded for her to continue.

"Okay. First we have to start with the victim. Ralph,

by all accounts, was lacking a bit in people skills. This left many people angry or at least not happy with him, but it doesn't account for anyone wanting to murder him."

She pointed to a diagram of the area of Ralph's back yard. "The scene of the murder." It showed the house, the compost pile, the wood pile, the lilac bushes separating their yards, the path to the forest trail, and the way to Kandi's house, including the garage and coop.

"Does this look accurate to everyone?"

They all nodded.

Carson stood motionless. Watching.

"Okay. Here is where Ralph's body was found." She pulled a translucent sheet over the white paper. This page had been marked with the location of Ralph's body on the compost pile. Several in the room cringed.

"Now let's begin with the timing of the events according to what has been shared thus far. Right after I moved in, I heard screaming coming from the next yard. When I arrived, I found Ralph telling Kandi to keep her chicken out of his tomatoes. He held an axe in one hand and Rusty's neck in the other. Kandi was holding Rusty and also clutching the axe. Her pushing back against Ralph explains how Kandi's fingerprints got on the axe handle. However…"

Anne threw a marker toward Kandi. "Catch!" Kandi grabbed the marker with her left hand.

"Kandi's left-handed. She was holding Rusty in her left hand and pushing on the axe with her right. If she had attacked Ralph with the axe, she would have most likely used her dominant hand." She took the marker back from Kandi.

Out of the corner of her eye, Carson threw a piece of crumpled-up paper at her. With her right hand holding the marker, she reached out and caught the paper with her left hand.

Drat. That man.

"Okay. Yes, technically you will use whatever hand is available but it's still something to consider, right?" She queried the sheriff who responded with a miniscule nod.

"Now let me continue. The thing was…Ralph had no intention of killing the chicken. He was simply finishing his morning's wood chopping." Anne took a quick look round the room, then continued.

"Then I arrived. As I backed up, my foot hit the moist compost. It was extremely slippery and before I knew it I'd fallen into the pile. Ralph set the axe down and he and Kandi helped me up. Well, for a bit, anyway." Kandi grinned at Anne's unspoken admonition.

Anne twisted to face Stewart. He scowled at her. "I'd spoken with Stewart about his uncle and he'd told me Ralph enjoyed his visits with Kandi. Truth be told, he could've easily put up a fence. Or used another method to stop the chicken from coming into his yard. But this was a way to interact with Kandi. Stewart said Ralph thought Kandi was a strong young woman. He was proud of her."

"Really?" Kandi turned to Stewart. "Is this true?"

Stewart nodded. "He thought you had a steel spine to have made it after your mama did what she did. He used to tell me, 'That girl has gumption. She'll achieve anything she wants if…'"

Kandi goaded him. "If what?"

"Um…I can't recall," Stewart stumbled.

Anne caught Stewart's poor attempt at an obvious lie. "Let me refresh your memory, Stewart. Might it have been something like, '…if she wasn't married to Jeff?'"

"Hey!" Jeff jumped from his seat. "What's the meaning of this?"

Stewart nodded.

Kandi patted Jeff's arm, but he swatted her hand away. "I don't have to listen to this."

Carson stepped forward. "Take a seat."

Jeff reluctantly obeyed.

Anne continued. "Store surveillance worked on Stewart's behalf. He'd parked his vehicle in a parking lot that captured him and his van on the night Ralph died. So Stewart is cleared." Anne drew a red X over his name.

Turning to face the computer screen, Anne addressed Eliza. "Eliza, I'm going to continue with you. You told me the other evening that you'd been taking a sleeping aid, then stopped. I looked it up on the internet. You can readily find that it's known to cause anxiety, walking and driving in your sleep, hallucinations, even homicidal or suicidal thoughts. That's also why you continued to carry out your morning jogging routine. It was an ingrained habit imprinted on your subconscious."

Eliza started to say something before her lawyer motioned her to stay quiet.

Anne went on. "Now, on the day in question, you rose at your normal time around five for your run. As usual, you had on your jogging outfit, a balaclava on your hair, and your gloves. As you ran on the forest path, a noise cut through your slumber-jog, for lack of a better word.

It was Ralph chopping wood. As an early riser, he liked to get in some work before the sun came up. Another habit. But this day was different."

She paused. "Because someone *else* was there that morning."

All eyes followed her as she turned toward Faith. Anne bent down in front of Faith. The elderly woman's eyes were bright.

Anne's voice was soft and soothing. "Faith, did you go visit Ralph?"

Faith took Anne's face in her hands. "He loved me, you know. He always loved me."

Anne nodded. "I know." She took the woman's fragile hands and placed them back in her lap. Hope edged closer to her mother.

Anne addressed Eliza. "I wish you could recall your entire 'dream'"—she made quotes in the air with her fingers—but this is what I think really happened. She grabbed a pencil and drew a dotted line on the vellum paper. "Faith was walking across the yard. She wore a felt cloche hat." She turned and spoke softly. "Hope?"

Hope lifted a brown paper sack from inside the bag she'd brought with her. Hesitating for a brief moment, she opened it to reveal a dark red hat. It lay crumpled, stained, and stiff. Underneath was what appeared to be a bloody cotton nightdress.

"I contacted Hope yesterday with my theory, and she shared with me about these items. She hadn't shared them before because she figured it had been an accident, and she had faith that Kandi would be proven innocent of the charges."

Carson immediately ordered the deputy to take the items from Hope. The deputy stood behind Hope and her mother. Hope addressed the group. "I'm sorry. We can't bring him back. What would it serve...I'm sorry, Kandi, I didn't—"

Anne interrupted. "Wait, Hope. As Paul Harvey used to say, we need to hear the rest of the story." She got the nod from Carson to continue. "As you can see, Faith is a very petite woman. It was dark, and she wore a hat that covered her gray hair. In a dreamlike state and at a distance, Eliza could have easily mistaken Faith for someone much younger. Maybe even, depending on the tricks of the mind—a younger sister."

Eliza let out a sob and brought her fist to her mouth in dismay.

"So Eliza, you're running. Through the opening into Ralph's yard you see a white man holding an axe. A young woman advancing. He moves toward her. You won't let him hurt her—not this time. You sprint to him. There's a struggle. Ralph, who's already in ill health, has a hard time fighting you off. He either throws the axe in the compost pile or it falls during the struggle. He pushes you away or you both collapse. From your description, the struggle resulted in you both being knocked out. However, for you, it may have actually knocked you into some wakefulness."

Anne faced Sam. "Am I correct that during your autopsy you found Ralph had also experienced a heart attack?"

Sam addressed the group. "Yes. It looks like he'd been having myocardial infractions for some time, but he must have simply disregarded them. During our investigation his doctor said he'd been complaining of chest pains. But he'd refused more testing."

She paused and looked at Carson. "Now I know that all of that is pure conjecture." He nodded an affirmative. Anne turned and spoke. "So with your lawyer's permission, Eliza, I'd like you to tell me and the others what you saw after you came to."

Eliza brushed off her lawyer's call to silence. "I don't know if it woke me up, but I certainly became conscious. Ralph was lying on the ground. His eyes were closed. Fear coursed through me. I was afraid I'd killed him. I ran."

"Thank you." Anne turned to Kandi. "Kandi, the next morning I came running over when I heard you screaming for help. Correct?"

Kandi swallowed and nodded.

Anne pulled another vellum sheet down over the other clear sheet. "Here's where I found Kandi kneeling by Ralph. Her hands were covered in blood. Kandi, please tell us what happened that morning. And this is already on the record. Right?" Anne spoke to the sheriff.

Carson nodded. "Correct."

Kandi gulped, and then steadied her voice. "Rusty had gone missing. I went to Ralph's to collect her before he got mad again. I saw Ralph lying on the compost pile."

"Wait. Stop there. *How* was he lying?"

"What do you mean?" Kandi tilted her head.

"Face up, facedown?" Anne flipped the palm of her hand.

"Oh, facedown."

Anne nodded. "Continue."

"I said, Ralph, did you do a face plant? You know, like what you did the other day, Anne." She chuckled, then became sober. "But he didn't respond. I turned him over and…that's when I saw all the blood. I must have tried to help him, but it was no use. He was dead. Then you showed up. I have a hard time remembering clearly after that."

"That's okay. What did you do with the axe?" Anne asked.

"The axe?" Kandi stared up at Anne.

"Yes. Why did you move it? Why put it in your own yard?"

"I didn't. I've said this over and over. There was *no* axe!"

Anne spoke to Eliza. "Did you take the axe?"

Eliza shook her head. "No. I just ran."

Anne saw she now had the sheriff's undivided attention, but his eyebrows were raised. He wasn't sold yet.

She turned back to Faith. "Faith, you loved Ralph very much."

Faith looked up at her. "Yes."

Anne hunched down next to the frail woman. "Faith, did you kill Ralph?"

Chapter Twenty-Two

Hope bristled. "Don't talk to my mother that way."

Faith patted Hope's hand. She raised her daughter's hand to her lips and kissed it. "He loved you so much."

The elderly woman smiled at Anne. "He was going to take me home. That woman in the TV"—she pointed at Eliza's face—"ran away. He was on the ground asleep. But then he woke up. He saw me kneeling next to him. He kissed my hand." She stroked her hand. Then she stopped.

The room was quiet when she continued. "He got up from the ground. He said he'd take me home. But he didn't. He kept moaning. He fell on the pile. I waited. But I started getting so cold." She paused. "I like cold ice cream."

Anne had to get answers quickly before Faith faded away. "Faith, what happened next?"

The woman gazed up at Anne. "I turned him over. He was so heavy. I saw the axe. I pulled my hat off and tried to stop the bleeding. It wouldn't stop. I used my hat and pulled the axe out."

Anne turned to Sam. "I think if you take that hat in

for testing, you'll find Ralph's blood on it. It's also the reason Faith's fingerprints weren't on the axe."

Sam nodded. "May also confirm the unidentified fibers we found on scene."

She turned back. Faith gaze was unfocused.

Oh no. Please let her stay lucid a bit longer. She took the woman's hand. "What did you do with the axe, Faith?"

"I turned him back over so he could sleep on his stomach. He could sleep there forever." She smiled. Faith's thoughts were becoming jumbled between fantasy and reality.

"What about the axe, Faith? Did you move it?" Anne implored.

"He uses his axe every day. I left it so he could chop wood. He likes to chop wood. Sometimes I go visit him while she's"—she motioned at Hope—"asleep." She bent her head and put a finger to her lips.

Anne stood up and stretched her back. She moved to the front of the room. "This is what I believe happened. Eliza, in a hallucination, thought she was saving Faith from a slave trafficker." Others in the room sucked in their breath at these words. "Eliza and Ralph struggled. Both fell, but neither was seriously hurt. Eliza came to first, thought Ralph was dead, and ran. However, when Ralph woke, he spied the axe in the compost pile. He either reached for it or then had a heart attack or both happened concurrently. He slipped, which I can tell you from firsthand experience is very easy to do when you're close to that pile. He then fell on the axe. It was a fluke accident that Ralph fell and hit the sharp edge."

She turned to Sam. "As our coroner, is this scenario plausible?"

"Yes. You wouldn't believe some of the things I've seen. People have all sorts of strange ways of killing themselves. I remember this one time—"

"Thanks, Sam." Anne didn't want to hear about the coroner's gruesome find. "So, Faith pulled the axe from Ralph, but he was mortally wounded. The axe had missed his chest and he'd fallen on his stomach. Sam can concur if the fatal wound hit one of Ralph's vital organs."

Sam cleared his throat and spoke clearly. "The wound penetrated Ralph's soft tissue as well as his intestines, kidney, and liver." He patted his abdomen. "As you all heard, Ralph had already been experiencing some heart issues. Since he didn't receive aid quickly, he succumbed to his injuries. Though I seriously doubt Ralph would have survived anyway. I'm fairly confident he would have had a fatal heart attack within the next few days. Big blockages in his arteries."

"Thanks, Sam." Anne turned back to the group. "As you just heard, Faith had taken the axe and put it next to the woodpile. She swiveled to face Hope. "When you went to get your mother that morning, was she in her bed?"

After taking a deep breath, Hope responded. "No, she wasn't in her bed. She was out on the back porch, rocking back and forth. She was crying and holding her hat. Her feet and gown were covered in mud and muck. At least I thought it was mud at the time. I stripped her clothing and put her in a bath. Then I heard mom saying strange things about Ralph. I ran over to see if he'd been hurt and that's when I saw everything. I realized then that her clothes were covered in blood. I knew she couldn't have killed him. So I stuck the items in a bag and I haven't touched them since. Later, I wondered if she had killed him because of his rejection of her all those years ago. But no matter what, I knew it would do no good for them to prosecute her."

Faith reached over and patted Hope on the head like a mother would do to a toddler. "Don't cry, baby. It's okay."

Carson motioned for Sam to escort Faith out of the room.

Anne looked back at the group. "All this time, Hope thought her mother had killed Ralph. But when she heard about Kandi, she thought that vindicated her mother. Correct?"

Hope nodded. She began weeping. "I'm sorry, Kandi. I didn't know what to do."

Anne spoke up. "But we have to go back to an important part of the story."

"The axe." The sheriff's voice echoed across the room.

"Yes." Anne nodded at the chief, who signaled for her to continue. "That is a major missing piece. If Kandi had killed Ralph, then why would she be stupid enough to hide the axe in her own yard, where it was bound to be found? It just didn't make sense." She smiled at the young woman. "I know Kandi. And she's a smart young lady. So why take the axe at all?" Anne scanned the group.

"Ralph died due to a tragic accident. But *someone* wanted to gain from his death." With a marker, Anne drew X's through names on the wall.

One name remained.

Jeff's fidgeting worsened. Kandi slowly turned from Anne to her husband and back. Anne spoke to Kandi. "I'm sorry, sweetie. I truly am." She reached behind a chair and uncovered a large black plastic bag. Inside, another clear plastic bag showed the outline of a dead chicken sans head. She then pulled out a freezer bag with a head in it. Rusty.

"Rusty!" Kandi teared up. "What? Where?"

"Kandi," Anne spoke softly to the crying woman. "What happens in a few months?"

"What do you mean?" Kandi wiped her eyes.

Anne waited.

"My inheritance." Kandi's voice rose. "*My* inheritance? Jeff? How could you!"

Anne spoke loudly and quickly. "You'd told Jeff about Ralph threatening Rusty. He doesn't care about your chickens. He made that evident the first time I met him. His trip had already concluded, and he'd decided to come home early. Unfortunately, he made the mistake of taking the shuttle, and of course, they keep records." Anne produced a piece of paper.

Jeff jumped from his seat, but the deputy put a hand on his shoulder and he sat back down.

Anne handed the paper to the sheriff. "As I said, Jeff had taken the red-eye. The shuttle dropped him off, and he decided to cut between Ralph's and his house instead of taking the long driveway to the back. That's where he spied Faith wandering the back yard in her bloody clothing. He's the one who found the axe where Faith had put it."

She turned to Jeff. "I bet you couldn't believe your luck. Here was your chance to get your hands on Kandi's money while she went to prison. You doubted Faith would even recall what she'd done—or at least what you *thought* she'd done. But you wanted to make sure that no one would doubt Kandi had done it. You hid the axe in the bushes, and *you* killed Rusty. Kandi had told you that she and Ralph had been arguing about the chickens in his garden. You know how much Kandi thinks of her chickens so it wouldn't be a stretch to convince others she could be capable of doing something rash to save them. Even a manslaughter charge over an accidental death could put Kandi away while you siphoned off her money. I couldn't figure out who had been messing with the compost pile since it had already been searched but you were trying to incriminate Kandi."

The tension in the air was palatable as the group stared at Jeff.

Kandi rose and moved to the chair next to Hope, who put her arm around the trembling woman's shoulders.

Anne addressed Carson. "I'd seen someone running from the yard before I got knocked out. It turned out to be a rake, not someone hitting me. But there hadn't been a rake there before. I wondered why. Then I remembered seeing something red there. But it had snowed so I wasn't able to see what it was. I recently went back and noticed that one side of the compost looked freshly turned. That's when I found Rusty's head." She scowled at Jeff. "You were going to bury her entirely, but I stopped that when I saw you that evening. Later, when I was in my attic, I saw you retrieve the rest of the hen from where you'd hidden her."

Anne stepped up to the diagram and drew a large circle by the woodpile of Kandi's garage. "Here." She glanced over at the sheriff. "I believe if you look in that area, you'll find evidence of the chicken, and possibly even some of Ralph's blood from the axe."

"Why you—" Stewart pulled Jeff up by his shirt front and punched him in the face. "How could you do that to Kandi?"

The deputy quickly pulled Stewart away and pinned his arms behind his back.

"I want this man arrested! He assaulted me. You all saw it!" Jeff wiped blood from his lip.

Kandi sobbed into her hands. "I can't believe it. I can't believe it."

"Oh, shut up your crying," Jeff spat. "I didn't kill the old guy. I saw him fall. Thought the old broad had killed him."

Hope rose from her seat, her face contorted in anger. "And you did nothing?"

Carson stepped forward and motioned for Hope to sit.

Jeff's incessant rant turned back to Kandi. "And who cares about a stupid chicken? You and all your dumb country stuff. I'm sick of it. I want a divorce."

Carson moved over and took Jeff by the arm.

"Hey! What're you doing?" Jeff tried to wrestle away from him, but Carson was much stronger.

"I think we need to go and have a little chat down at the station."

"About what?"

"Let's see. How about for starters—tampering with a possible murder scene, obstruction of justice, attempt to commit larceny, trespassing. I'm sure I'll think of some others. Let's go."

He nodded to Anne. "Good job, Nancy Drew. Come visit me tomorrow and we'll work through this idea of yours."

"What about Eliza?"

"She still has to go through the system." He pointed to Jeff. "Deputy."

The deputy escorted Jeff out of the room.

"Thank you, thank you." Eliza's voice cut through the strange silent left by their absence.

Anne had forgotten that Eliza and her lawyer were watching on the computer screen. "Yes, Ms. Freemont," the lawyer intoned, "I believe you have certainly helped our case if nothing more than to establish reasonable doubt." Without any further comment, the screen went blank.

After all the other people had left, Sorcha entered the room carrying a tray. She poured tea into a mug. "Sit here."

Kandi obeyed.

"I'm so stupid. I'm always so stupid. I thought he loved me." She sobbed.

Sorcha pushed the cup into Kandi's hands. "Drink." She poured another cup and handed it to Anne. After providing herself with a cup, Sorcha settled onto a nearby chair. She toasted Anne. "You did it. Your theory seems the most plausible, and the facts seem to go together."

"I just wanted to help Kandi."

Kandi looked up from where she'd been staring into her cup. Suddenly, she spat out, "I hate you. Everything was fine until you came. You've ruined my life. I never want to see you again."

"But, Kandi, she helped—" Sorcha started.

"Helped what? Ruin my marriage? Make Jeff want to divorce me?" She broke down crying into her hands again.

Sorcha spoke softly to Anne, "I think you better leave."

Anne set her cup on the table. Outside she went through the motions of starting her car and steering it home.

Maybe this isn't the place for me after all. It's been nothing but trouble and heartache.

She drove home in a daze. On her back porch, she collapsed in a chair, where she cried for everything she'd lost and for what would never be. The clearing of a man's throat startled her. Sam. She wiped her face with her hands. She took in a deep breath as he joined her on the porch.

"Come here." He enveloped her in his warm embrace. "I just heard from Sorcha. She's worried about you. She told me what Kandi said." He pulled her away so as to look in her face. "You have to know Kandi doesn't mean it. She's just hurt right now and had to take it out on someone. Unfortunately, you're that someone."

He pulled her close again. "It will work out. Don't worry. Now let's get you inside. It looks like it might rain." Opening the door, he led her into the kitchen.

"Get some sleep. Don't make any rash decisions. I'm taking the evidence over to the medical examiner's office today. I also think Eliza may be able to make bond. We'll see how good her lawyer is." He bent down and kissed her on the cheek. "It'll work out. Trust me."

The morning found Anne walking through the house, envisioning what she'd thought of doing when things seemed brighter. She trudged to the attic and opened the shutters. Crime investigators hovered around Kandi and Jeff's wood pile and next to the garage where a line of crime scene tape marked off the area. In Ralph's yard, another group secured the path to the forest, the wood pile, and the area leading to Kandi's house. She turned from the window. She'd seen enough.

Reaching the first floor, she heard a light tapping on her back door. She wasn't going to answer it. They could all go away. But then she noticed the red hair. Kandi. She opened the door.

The girl flew into her arms. "I'm sorry. I shouldn't have said that. Please forgive me."

Anne broke down in tears. "I'm sorry too. I didn't mean to hurt you. I just wanted you to know the truth about Jeff."

"I know. I know. It's just hard having the fact that

your husband never really loved you thrown in your face in front of everyone."

Don't I know it.

"Please sit down. You want some coffee?"

"Yes. Thanks. Here, let me help." Before Anne could stop her, Kandi was pulling out the coffee beans and grinding them. Anne's stomach growled. Then Kandi's. They glanced at one another, then broke out in laughter that filled the room. "I gather you didn't eat anything last night either."

"No. But I'm hungry now!"

"Breakfast burritos okay with you?"

"Yes. That sounds great."

Anne pulled eggs, cheddar cheese, bacon, salsa, and tortillas from the fridge. The pair shared companionable silence as they prepared and ate their meal.

"This hits the spot. I didn't realize how hungry I was." Anne took a swig of coffee.

"Me too." Kandi's voice lowered. "They've arrested Jeff. I guess he, *like*, got scared with all the possible charges Sheriff Carson alluded to. He did move the axe into our yard, and he killed Rusty. That bum. He had all kinds of excuses. That he had no choice. His company is in really bad straits. He said he figured I'd get out of the murder charges, but I believe that as far as I can, *like*, throw him. Turns out he'd been embezzling money, and he hadn't been able to pay it back. He's going away for a long time."

"I'm sorry, Kandi. Really." *Not really. Good riddance to bad rubbish.*

"I think I'm the only person who didn't see him for who he really was."

"I resemble that remark."

Kandi laughed heartily. "I guess you do, at that. It's probably why you could see through all his bull." She shoved the last bite of burrito into her mouth.

"But first, I don't want to ever hear you say that you're stupid. You're not stupid. You're a brilliant, talented young woman. Some people have treated you badly but that isn't a reflection on you. It's a reflection on them. Okay?"

"*Like*, okay." Kandi grinned.

"Ugh, I'm going to, like, strangle you, if you say like one more time!" Anne retorted.

Chapter Twenty-Three

Anne used her toes to rock back and forth in the old rocker, a cup of steaming coffee clutched in her hands. She took a sip and sighed with contentment. Though early morning, the sun's warmth enveloped the back porch. She rubbed the worn wooden arm of the chair. The rockers, which had once sat on Ralph's porch, had been Hope's gift to Anne.

She glanced at the town newspaper beside her. The headline stood out. Eliza de French cleared of all charges. The article went into how the medical examiner confirmed Ralph's heart condition and undiagnosed diabetes. They surmised that low blood sugar and exertion caused Ralph to black out. Forensics alleged Ralph had already been unstable when he reached for the axe in the compost pile. His poor health would have caused death to occur fairly soon even without the incident.

As for Eliza, by the time Ralph woke up, she was already home. To corroborate her story, another jogger swore under oath Eliza ran past him. The timing of that encounter placed her away from Ralph's house when the actual death occurred.

After the police confirmed Ralph's death was an unfortunate accident, the town had breathed a collective sigh of relief. The idea of a killer in their midst might make for good press and curiosity seekers, but it left everyone else on edge. The once open town had begun locking their doors at night and, sadly, Anne didn't know if they would ever go back. But for now, everyone radiated high spirits.

Except Kandi.

Deciding to give their marriage one last chance, Kandi had traveled to the correctional facility in Denver to see Jeff. But on arrival, she'd been informed his wife was already there. Not only had Jeff been cheating his company, but the rumors of another woman had turned out to be true.

While Anne's heart broke for Kandi, she took comfort in the fact Jeff would never hurt the young women ever again. His actions had hammered the final nail in the coffin of Kandi's relationship with him. And coupled with his embezzling, Jeff would be going to prison for a very long time.

Sunlight crept backward across the porch. Anne watched it retreating. How long had she been sitting here? She stared across the yard. Observing.

Anne quoted aloud, "The first rule of permaculture is to observe." Well, she'd been doing that for the last week. She'd come to love sitting on the back porch, the rocking cadence a calming influence. In the morning, she'd grab a trusty quilt and head outside to drink her morning brew as the world awoke.

Anne took a deep breath.

What about you then? Are you ready to give love another chance? Or have you closed off your heart forever?

No. I'm just not ready.

So when will you be ready? Next month? Next year? Ever?

Anne sighed deeply. Nothing worse than fighting with yourself.

She didn't want to struggle anymore. She wanted to live life to the fullest. Her thoughts turned to Ralph. Anne recalled her spills into the compost pile. Fluke accidents happen every day. Disease can creep up on you. Life can end quickly.

A tear slid down her cheek.

Oh, geez. Why am I crying? Not the hormones again.

Anne cradled her chin in her hands as a multitude of feelings ran through her.

She *had* fallen in love.

In a way she had never expected.

But she had. Anne had fallen in love with this town and its inhabitants. And with one person in particular.

What to do about it?

Well, that's just plain crazy.

So what—you're crazy!

Anne made up her mind. Afraid and giddy at the same time, she was going to do the most reckless thing she'd ever done. But first, she needed to make some plans. An idea finally occurred to her. She'd host a housewarming party.

A warm breeze had carried away the crispness of the morning. It wouldn't be much longer before winter would truly embrace them. The timing was perfect for an end of season outdoor party.

Stewart waved at her as he escorted a young lady Anne hadn't seen before. "Hey, Anne, great party."

"Thanks." She raised her glass.

Butterflies flitted in her stomach.

Was she really going to go through with this? Could she? In front of all these people? What if she made a fool of herself for all time? Well—said her inner critic—*it's not like you haven't done that already a few times.*

She took a sip of her mimosa. Then another.

Anne looked out at the group assembled. In the short time that she'd live in Carolan Springs, she'd gotten to know quite a few of its inhabitants. She glanced over to a table heaping with jams, jellies, and other preserved foods; quilts and knitted goods from the local ladies society; books from Sorcha; lotions and potions from Hope; and gardening gloves and beautiful pottery dishware from Eliza. Garlic and onions, some for eating and some for planting, poked out of various buckets. A box full of freshly picked produce and late season berries sat off in the shade.

Some of the gifts had been a bit tongue-in-cheek such as a set of compost bins from Stewart, chocolate cherry candies from Kandi, and a set of Nancy Drew books from Sheriff Carson.

Anne felt loved.

She moved among the crowd, talking with her guests. Music from a local folk band floated across the air, mingling with the sounds of joyful chatter and laughter. Much of the food had been eaten and people were happy and content. Anne surveyed the crowd.

Now or never.

Anne willed herself to stop shaking.

She glanced to where Kandi, Sam, Sorcha, and Carson stood talking. Across from them, she spied Stanley. The old man winked at her. Of all the people in town, Anne had gone to him with her idea. When she told him, he hadn't smirked once. Even better, he told her to go for it.

Anne strode to the porch and stood on the top step facing the crowd. The music died down. She threw back her shoulders and cleared her throat.

Everyone waited.

She swallowed hard and willed herself to speak. "Thank you for coming. I'm grateful to have moved to a place with such wonderful people. I'm appreciative of all the friends I've made here, and hope to get to know each of you better in the days ahead."

Someone yelled, "To Anne." Everyone chimed in and took a drink.

"Um, yes. Thank you." Anne found Stanley in the crowd. He gave her a thumbs-up.

"I…I…well, to say these last few months have been a crazy introduction to this town might be an understatement."

Everyone laughed.

"But it's because of the tragedy—"

"To Ralph," someone shouted.

"To Ralph," others echoed the words.

This was getting off track fast.

"Yes, to Ralph." She raised her glass, took a sip, and then set it down on the railing. She grasped her hands together to stop the shaking. There was no turning back now. Hopefully she wasn't about to become the town fool.

"Anyway. As I was saying, it's been during this time that I've really gotten to know many of you."

She paused. "And it seems that I…I…have lost my heart to one of you in particular."

This is it. Just do it. Don't think.

She turned.

"I never thought that I could care for someone the way I do for you. I thought that I had lost the chance to ever experience this type of love. But I've found out that I *am* able to feel it. Kandi, I could never replace your mother, but I know in my heart that I love you like I would love my own daughter. You once said that it would take the impossible to believe I'd never abandon you. Well, I hope to prove it to you."

Anne got down on one knee and pulled a box from her pocket. Inside, the little box held two pink booties. "Will you do me the honor of being my daughter and allowing me to adopt you? I promise to never leave you …" she said through tears and laughter, "unless I fall into a compost pile and die."

Kandi clutched her hands to her chest. Tears streamed

down her cheeks. "I'd be honored for you to be my mother. Yes! Yes, of course!"

The audience shouted and clapped as the two women embraced.

An elderly woman wiped her eyes. "Oh my, that's just the sweetest thing I ever did see."

One of the ladies from the woman's auxiliary chimed in, "Bless her heart."

A guy standing next to her said, "That's just dumb. She's a grown woman. You don't adopt a grown-up."

The woman batted him with her large purse.

"Hey!" He frowned and moved off, clutching his empty beer bottle.

"Men," the other lady quipped.

The band struck up a lively tune. Kandi and Anne were enveloped by the crowd who showered them with well wishes. Hugs and tears were in abundance.

Anne had not just found the home she'd always dreamed about but the daughter she'd always wanted.

From the Author

I hope you enjoyed reading *Chicken Culprit*. Would you mind doing me a big favor and reviewing it on Amazon, Goodreads or wherever you share what you're reading? I'd appreciate it!

Are you interested in backyard farming or what I call it—suburban homesteading? If so, then get tips through my

Homesteading Facebook page:
https://www.facebook.com/havensteader

Also, you can check out my author page:
https://www.facebook.com/VikkiWaltonAuthor

Finally, you can contact me directly:
vikki@vikkiwalton.com

Like everyone says, you may write alone, but it takes a lot of people to help you reach the finished product. Even with all their expertise, any errors you may find are all mine.

Hilary LaBarre, Deputy Coroner—who knew talking about gory deaths could be so much fun!

The Misplaced Modifiers—especially Donita and Jill—who improved the story with their insights.

Erica of Ink Deep Editing, who made editing less painful and caught development issues I'd missed.

Melinda of Martin Publishing Services who went the extra mile on helping me bring this book to fruition.

Erika Parker Rogers for her artistic talent.

Lt. Jane of the Colorado Springs Police Department who explained evidence requirements to make an arrest; then said with a serious tone, "Now don't go committing any murders."

Any errors you find are mine—all mine.

Finally to my kiddos, Michelle, Matthew, Jeremiah, and Jori, and to my husband, Jack, who puts up with me.